trust
& betrayal

trust
& betrayal

real life
stories of
friends and
enemies

by Janet Bode

Published by
Bantam Doubleday Dell Books for Young Readers
a division of
Bantam Doubleday Dell Publishing Group, Inc.
1540 Broadway
New York, New York 10036

ISBN 0-440-22035-1

Reprinted by arrangement with Delacorte Press

Printed in the United States of America

January 1997

10 9 8 7 6 5 4 3 2 1

to
Judy Senn Pollock
Kay Dougherty Franey

contents

trust
& betrayal

getting along

This started out to be a book on withstanding peer pressure. But as I crisscrossed the country, teenagers kept telling me that that was an issue adults worried about.

A teenager from Kansas even said he was tired of hearing the expression "peer pressure." He suggested we ought to call it "socially challenged." The other students laughed and agreed.

They also agreed that their real concern with peer relations was not who pressured whom, but who got along with whom and who didn't. These complex relationships caused all of them problems at one time or another. In fact, that was the issue they wanted to explore.

They began to offer examples of how they acted and interacted with friends, enemies, and strangers their age. For a year I taped and transcribed individual stories. As my collection grew, I would tell students from one state some of the accounts I was hearing in others.

For instance, there was the loner who had no friends, and no one at school bothered to wonder why. Another story was about two best girlfriends who let a boy destroy their once-solid friendship.

A self-described "easy target," picked on and tor-

mented by his peers, discussed life from his point of view.
A poetry-writing drug dealer did the same thing, as well as
a voluptuous redhead who was the target of too much
male attention.

Another teenager spoke of anger toward her friends
when they wanted off the emotional roller coaster she'd
put them on during her multiple suicide attempts.

Three students from one school explained their differ-
ing impressions of what happened when a nineties issue
threatened to tear their student body apart.

After I related these stories, the students in the middle
schools and high schools I visited discussed their reactions
to each slice-of-life view. I took notes as they told me how
they might act in a similar situation. What advice would
they give? What did they look for in a friend? Did the
teens in these examples share their values?

Then I asked, "If you have a story you want to tell,
please let me know." When students volunteered, I added
their names to my list of interview sources.

Throughout this process, I also checked with adults
who worked with teenagers. I wanted their interpreta-
tion of peer relations. "What's going on here," I asked,
"and what can others learn from these individual accounts?"

trust & betrayal is a selection of the stories I gathered in those many conversations. Yes, the language you
read is often raw and choppy. The grammar isn't perfect,

either. The tenses even switch from past to present and back again.

But as much as possible, I wanted you to hear the teenagers' voices as I heard them. In addition, before I turned on the tape recorder, I'd remind them that their words weren't mainly intended for me or other adults. Instead, as they answered my questions, they should envision a peer in whom they would confide.

I think they did.

Now come along with me for a glimpse into the real lives of teenagers. Their tales are meant to entertain you. They are also meant to provoke you, to make you evaluate your own interactions.

Human connections take care and nurturing. We don't always take the time to think about how we behave toward others. At best, some of us convince ourselves that tolerance is a goal, not just a stop on the journey to understanding. At worst, we cause others enormous pain. This might be the time to figure out where you fit in.

Some of the stories are followed by comments. They are a guide to get you started in considering whether you agree with how your peers handle difficult situations.

Here's a final comment. You don't have to read this book from beginning to end. Surf through the pages. Skim the titles and the pullouts, the words printed in the boxes. Then start with any section that brings out a strong response in you.

Once you've finished, if you'd like to share your stories, please write to me at the address below.

JANET BODE
c/o Delacorte Press
1540 Broadway
New York, New York 10036

linda

no friends allowed

As soon as my mom married my stepdad, he expected me to call him Dad. And he started to run my life, especially when it came to friends. I couldn't have any.

I'd ask, "Can I please have a girlfriend over?"

"No," he'd say, "there's work to be done."

"Can I stay after school?"

"No," he'd say, "you have things to do around here." He always had some excuse why.

My mother would hear and say, "It's unfair." Then they'd argue some. At first I wondered why she didn't argue more. Now, I think that Mom knew if they had fought anymore that what eventually happened would have happened sooner.

I believe she was scared to death for me, and for herself.

As time went by, I stopped asking and just hid my feelings inside. That, and I prayed. Mom always said, "When you feel you have nobody else on earth to talk to, at least you can pray about things. That will help you."

At school I kept very much to myself. I convinced myself my goal was to learn, not to make friends. Sometimes I'd think about what it would be like to have a best girlfriend. But I tried not to let it bother me. I tried not to be lonely. I guess you could say I got used to it.

my secrets

I become involved in some clubs. Since I'm not allowed to stay after school, I join the ones that meet before classes. That makes me look like I'm a social person. But I'm not really.

People never call me on the phone or go anywhere with me. I talk to them a little, especially a girl named Jeanne. I wish I could tell her why I have to be this way. I wish that Jeanne or any one of them might reach out and try to get me to tell them my secrets. I worry, "They probably think I'm supershy or worse yet—weird."

Then one day this guy Timothy notices me. He smiles. Somehow he gets my number and calls. When my stepdad answers the phone, he doesn't say, "Hold on a minute." He just slams down the receiver. Timothy calls again.

This time my stepdad still doesn't say, "Hold on a minute," but he does yell for me. I nearly faint. Timothy says, "I got the idea to call you and keep calling until you talked to me."

"Well, I'm talking to you, aren't I?" I say.

"I saw you at school and started asking people about you. Everybody said, 'I don't know much about Linda. She doesn't say much. But she seems nice.'"

"Thankyouthankyou," I think to myself.

To Timothy I say, "I admire your persistence." And then he asks me out. It's the end of my junior year in high school. It shouldn't be a big deal. But how can it not be? At the least, maybe I can have my first friend.

Instead, the arguments between my mom and my stepdad about me start again. I can hear my mom say, "I am absolutely not going to let Linda spend her whole high school years not even dating." Finally, my stepdad gives in.

I go out with Timothy three times. I start to open up to him just a touch. There are worlds, though, that I can't let him enter.

> I worry, ''They probably think I'm supershy or worse yet— weird.''

The fourth time we go out it's to a football game. The new rule is, okay, I can go, but I have to be home by ten, in bed by ten-thirty, and up ready by seven A.M. to do chores the next morning.

I do all that. But my stepdad lies to my mother. "Linda didn't get home until two," he tells her. "She shouldn't be able to see Timothy anymore."

He makes up other things to trick my mother into thinking I shouldn't be with Timothy.

He and my mother fight again and again. She keeps saying, "That wouldn't be fair."

On a Monday morning my stepdad comes into my bedroom and says, "What do you think you're doing?"

"Getting ready for school," I say.

"I told you before, you're not allowed to wear makeup or fix your hair."

I can tell he's upset.

I say, "I'm seventeen years old. I make straight A's. I never do anything wrong. Why don't you let me do the normal things everybody else does? Why do you punish me like this?"

I start walking toward the door. The bus is waiting. I don't want to miss it. My stepdad has a different plan. He pushes me down the stairs, then runs in front of me and slaps me so hard that when I get to school his hand mark's still on my face.

Timothy meets me at the bus stop and says, "What happened?"

I'm not scared to tell him, but I am embarrassed. I know I'm not the only teenager with this kind of home. And I know I have one thing going for me: my mom. I think in a lot of homes where abuse happens, both parents are indifferent.

I always know my mom really loves me.

I tell Timothy a few details, the beating, the rules about no friends. I think all along he suspects. After that, he knows.

He starts telling me more about his life. His mother left the family when he was young. I think, in a sense, he always needed a mother figure, and I needed a father figure.

We are so alike, yet in important ways we are different. He has a good relationship with his dad. When we met, he and my mother took to each other. He says, "I wish I had a mother like yours."

I'm a nurturing person. I want to take care of him. I need somebody to take care of me, too. There isn't any question from there on out. We are meant for each other.

In all this, what is just as great is I feel I finally have a friend.

unhappy too long

My mom sat me down and said, "Linda, your stepdad's pushed me around for the last time. I've told him to get out." I knew that time had been serious. She ended up in the hospital. She reported him to the police.

"I want him to go through therapy," she said. "He told me he doesn't have any money. I said I'd pay for it." She always felt sorry for him. I think that was why she married him. He had had a bad family life. She thought she could help him.

"Now, Linda, we need to help ourselves. We need to come out of this, to live as well as we can knowing what we've been through."

We live in a town of fifty thousand. That morning I woke up to discover that their fight made the local paper. Along with the story, they used some horrible photos:

My mom with a battered face, holding her broken arm.

The police with drawn guns.

My dad in handcuffs, screaming bloody murder.

I was embarrassed about going to school. Everybody might know. But then, since I had a different name than my mother and my stepfather, most people didn't make the connection. And since Timothy was my only friend, there wasn't talk about it.

After a few days had gone by, I suddenly realized, wow, my stepdad was gone! Yes! I'd been isolated and unhappy too long. Now, maybe, I could have a normal life, even a girlfriend or two.

I didn't know exactly how to go about making friends, but I said to myself, "Don't just sit around and wait for people to come to you. Start talking to them. Ask them to go out or come over."

So that's what I did. People were kind of shocked at first. I worried, "Maybe they'll think, 'What's her problem? Linda never talked to me before. Why would she want to talk to me now?' "

But I kept on starting conversations. Asking them about normal teenager stuff. I was in the bathroom when I overheard two girls, their names were Connie and Samantha, talking about me.

Connie was saying, "I don't get Linda. One day she doesn't say a word. The next she's calling, asking me to go places with her."

Samantha said, "I think Linda's stuck on herself 'cause she's so beautiful."

I couldn't believe what I heard. I didn't feel I was somehow better. At the same time I never dreamed anybody considered me beautiful. When I told Timothy, he smiled and said, "You are beautiful, outside and inside. Keep talking to people, see what else you learn."

I kind of understood that, during the past year we'd been together, I'd put pressure on him. Whenever my stepdad let me out, I wanted Timothy to spend all his time with me. It had become a problem.

He felt he had to take care of me. I guess, I got used to that. I expected it. We both knew if I had other friends, he could go off, and have more friends, too.

I called up Jeanne to ask her about a homework assignment. Another time I sat next to her during lunch. Then we talked after a club meeting. Little by little we started being fairly close. Finally she said to me, "We thought you hated us. You didn't want anything to do with us."

"Oh, that's so far from the truth," I said. "I was scared of my stepdad. He ran my life."

She looked sort of surprised, but then she surprised me and said, "Linda, would you like to try to join my sorority?"

a tragedy

I'm at school. A student aide comes from the office. I have a call. It's a friend of my mother's. "There's been a tragedy," she says. "Your mother's dead."

I can't believe what I'm hearing. "There was a struggle. It went on for fifteen to twenty minutes. Your mom fought back. She tried hard to get to the telephone."

"Who did it? Do they know who did it?"

There's nothing for what seems like eternity. Then she says, "Your stepdad showed up. His original story was, 'Well, it looks like somebody robbed the place.' After the police got him to the side, they started really questioning him. He admitted he did it. 'Self-defense,' he said. Your mother attacked him."

By then I'm hysterical. How can she be telling me this over the phone? Why can't she at least do it in person? Obviously she's wrong. She's forgotten to say my mom's in the hospital. Fighting for her life.

But, of course, she isn't.

My mom is dead.

It's seven months later. I'm living with my aunt and uncle so I don't have to move away. No one knows what to do to help me. They never had anything like this happen to them. Neither have I.

Timothy brings Jeanne over. She says, "Anytime you

want to go out, be by ourselves and talk about things, I'm here."

"I wonder, 'Why me.' I lie in bed at night and cry."

"You're human," she says.

"Let us help you, Linda," Timothy says. "Lots of the students wanted to go to the funeral. Send flowers and cards. They just didn't know you enough. They didn't know how you'd react."

I say, "Thanks for being there for me. My life's been a blur. The trial. My stepdad's confession. Still, I can't keep acting the way I've been acting."

"I want you to be my friend," Jeanne says.

"Me, too," I tell her. "I want you to be my friend."

Right then the phone rings. I can hear my aunt get it. Two minutes later she comes into the room and says, "That was your stepdad. From jail. He said he wanted to tell you he was sorry. I said, 'Sorry doesn't mean much to Linda. Leave her alone.' "

What do you think?

"*Linda has to be comfortable with the fact that what happened wasn't her fault. It's hard to forget and hard to learn to trust people.*"

—student, Terry Parker High School, Jacksonville, Florida

"*I hope I would have tried to be nice to Linda back when her stepfather wasn't letting her have friends. Usually if I take the time to understand someone else, I end up liking them.*"

—student, Phoenix High School, Roseburg, Oregon

adam and chip

never go down alone

Two Kansas high school seniors answer a student
interviewer's question about peer pressure.

Adam: Adults think that peer pressure for teenagers is
when somebody is standing there shoving a beer in our
face. The reality is that when I'm at a party and stuff, I
don't want to share my alcohol.

Chip: Yeah. After having to get other people's parents
to buy it for us or paying people outside liquor stores or
finding older brothers and sisters to go in instead, I want
the drink for myself. You know, this one's all mine.

Question: Do you do drugs because of peer pressure?

Adam: I do drugs because I want to be gone. It has
nothing to do with peer pressure. I was in a group where
nobody did drugs. Then one day it got so bad that I de-

cided I'd do drugs. I sought out the people who'd know where I could get them.

Chip: Most of what I do is because I want to do it anyway and don't want to feel guilty. But my rule for life is never go down alone. I pressure other people to do things with me. That way if I'm caught, I can always say, "Hey, it wasn't totally my fault."

Adam: I'm pressured more by people I don't know well. With close friends, if they want me to do something, I can say, "Screw you. I'm not doing that." With others, maybe I want to become better friends. Or I want to make a good impression. I don't want them to think I'm a loser.

Chip: Remember when we were freshmen? We'd see the seniors doing certain things and we'd think, "That's cool. We can do that once we get older." But sometimes I didn't want to wait. I'd think, "If I start now, I'm more of an adult."

Adam: What I remember from four years of high school is far more pressure from parents to do well than peers to do bad. That means more need to cheat on tests and homework than to drink or do drugs.

What do you think?

"Studies show you don't start to use drugs, shoplift—whatever—because of a pressure situation. Instead, it's two or three kids deciding together that this is what you want to do. And you do something you wouldn't necessarily do on your own.

"When a new friendship starts, you look for something you both enjoy doing, a 'common ground activity.' That's normal. The trouble starts if you find yourself in a relationship that tends to support things that aren't healthy for you."

—Tom Dishion, Ph.D., clinical psychologist, Oregon Social Learning Center, Adolescent Transitions Program, Eugene

kristi

friends again?

My best friend, Stephanie, and I were sitting in my bedroom. She's, like, "I don't want you to get mad. And I'm sorry I haven't told you this before. But you are the first person to know. . . ."

We'd sat and talked in my bedroom so many times since my family first moved to Oregon. As soon as we pulled up to the driveway to start unpacking, Stephanie came up and introduced herself.

"I live right down the street," she said.

I was shy back then. I was in sixth grade. She was a year older. She went up to my mom and said, "Do you need any help?"

It seems that within days Stephanie and I became best friends. We learned everything about each other. She never ignored me for her other friends.

In seventh grade, eighth grade, I'd still be over at her house for hours and hours. My mom would be calling, "Come home, Kristi."

"Give us another hour. We're still talking," I'd tell her. She'd end up calling again.

Anyway, Stephanie was sitting there saying, "Kristi, I don't know how to tell you, but I need your help."

"Just talk to me," I told her, because at the same time she's crying.

She said, "I'm five months pregnant and I don't know what to do."

I was surprised. I didn't really know what to say. I was, like, "What? Maybe you should tell your mom."

She said, "Kristi, you know she's always saying, 'If you ever get pregnant, I'm going to kill you.'"

"Stephanie, your mom won't kill you. She's just saying that to scare you. My mom tells me that, too."

"You don't know my mom," she said. "She will kill me. What do you think about an abortion?"

"Abortion! I can't believe you even thought it. It's killing another person. It's ignorant. You better not!"

Well, we talked and cried and talked. "Who's the father?" I said.

"Drew," she said, her boyfriend who didn't like me. I never knew why. I didn't like him, either. I wondered why she could tell me everything about her life, except that she was messing around with her boyfriend?

telling the secret

That night I had to get it off my back. I told my mom. She said, "When we first met Stephanie, she didn't seem like a person who would go out and get pregnant."

"I guess you never know, Mom."

"Kristi, if you ever get pregnant while you're in school, you're not living at my house."

I heard her, but I really didn't think she would do that.

"Is Stephanie embarrassed about this whole thing?" my mom said.

"Not that I know of," I said. "Maybe she hopes her parents will pay more attention to her if she has a baby."

As soon as Stephanie did tell her mom, she came back over to me.

"She just said, 'I knew this was going to happen.' "

"See," I said, "I told you she wouldn't kill you."

"Thank you for, like, encouraging me to tell her," Stephanie said, then she started hugging me.

"You know what's my real problem now," she said. "Drew is going out and getting drunk. He won't be with me all the time during my pregnancy. But Mike is."

Mike was Drew's best friend. He was up at her house all the time to support her. A week later she said to me, "I think I'm going to break up with Drew. But maybe I'll try to keep Mike in my life."

the strange silence

I didn't see Stephanie for a while. Then one day I was walking to my house and I saw her with Mike at the corner. I ran over, really upset, and said, "Where've you been?"

She said, "I had the baby. A girl, Chloe."

I said, "Well, how is she?" Stephanie started crying. "I had to have a C-section. Plus the baby was premature. She has to stay in the hospital a month longer. I'll probably spend most of my time there, too."

I said, "Look, I'll stop over later." I didn't know if there were things she'd tell me if Mike wasn't there. I waited about an hour and went over to her house. I said, "Stephanie, what's wrong?"

I guess he was jealous that Stephanie was dumping him for Mike.

"Oh, Kristi," she said and she started to cry. Then she tried to talk again. "Drew came into the hospital and ended up tearing up the maternity floor. He punched walls in!"

I wasn't surprised that Drew had been such a fool. I guess he was jealous that Stephanie was dumping him for Mike. Still, with a brand-new baby and everything, I didn't know what had gotten into her. She had better slow down.

And that's when everything between us started falling

apart. When the baby finally came home, Stephanie stayed in the house all the time.

She quit school.

She didn't have to. All people said was, "Another fifteen-year-old who doesn't know how to use her head."

I understood why the baby would be more important to her. But from then on for the next one whole year she didn't talk to me.

I wondered all the time, why? I asked her brother. He just said, "I don't know. She's become real weird."

I pushed him. I said, "Why's she doing this to me?"

He said, "I don't know, Kristi."

I called her mother. She said, "Stephanie never talks to anyone. I guess she's trying to be a good mother."

Once I saw her come back with her mom from the grocery store with baby food. But that was it. No more hours of conversations. No more running back and forth between our houses. No more friendship after three or so years.

the missing pieces

The summer before tenth grade, there's a knock at my door. My mom goes, "Kristi, Stephanie's here."

Nothing for nearly a solid year and now she comes to my house. I say, "What do you want?"

She's, like, "We have to talk."

"You want to talk now? Why?"

"We have a lot of things to talk about."

"Where's your baby and your boyfriend?"

"My mom has the baby and my boyfriend is another story. Why don't we go talk?"

"Okay."

Once we sit down, she says, "I'm real sorry for this past year when I haven't talked to you."

"What came over you to do all this?"

She says, "I don't know."

I say, "Is it Drew or Mike or your parents?"

She says, "It's me. I'm really stupid for ignoring you."

"You bet you are. Why did you do it?"

"Kristi," she says, "I have something to tell you."

"Well, what?"

"Four months after I had Chloe, I got pregnant again. I ended up having an abortion with that one."

"Was it Drew or Mike?" I say.

"It doesn't matter," she says.

"You're right. What matters is you committed murder. Leave my house. I don't want to talk to you."

She says, "But I had to do it."

I say, "Yeah, right."

She says, "Mom doesn't know. The only people who know are you and my Aunt Betty."

"Why'd you do it?"

"I already had Chloe. I didn't want to be a parent twice. Especially so soon together."

"Why didn't you just put it up for adoption?"

"You don't know how my feelings were. That would have hurt worse, never knowing."

I say, "Well, you still could have come to me before you got it done."

"I was too upset."

"No, the truth is you didn't want to hear what I'd say. You didn't want me in your life."

"I promise this won't happen again," she says.

I go, "Okay, we'll see how long this friendship lasts now."

the new picture

That night I talk this over with my mom and a couple other friends. They tell me, "Give her a chance." I think about it. Just all of a sudden becoming friends again will be hard.

I talk to her mom. She says, "Stephanie has lost all her friends. She needs somebody she can trust."

I say, "I think I can deal with that."

Starting a friendship again isn't like one, two, three. Stephanie and I go slowly. Sometimes we take the baby for a walk and

" If you can't be friends with your friends,

talk and talk. We try to figure out, why did we end up
not being friends?

Then she goes to her
house and I go to mine and
think some more.

I ask about Drew.
"How does he treat you
now? Does he do things for
you?"

"Not really."

"Does he help with
Chloe?"

"Not really."

"Well, why are you
with him? You know our

> it's going to
> be worse yet
> dealing with
> your ene-
> mies.''

friendship might have still been together if you had figured that out a long time ago."

She says, "I'm sorry. You know how I am."

I know. She still loves Drew to death. She does. Mike
is out of the picture entirely. And now she tells me she's
seeing this other guy, Tommy. She calls Drew "a friend."
She calls Tommy "Daddy." She's been with him for about
six months.

In all our figuring we finally get to why, exactly, she
didn't call me. Why she couldn't walk down the street
to see me. This is how I think the pieces fall into place:
She didn't want to see me or anybody, because she didn't

know what to do with her life. In a way she was embarrassed.

She was a fifteen-year-old having a baby. It's not that unusual, but most often you just don't want it to be you. It doesn't ever make your life easier.

She never told me why she came over that day and knocked on my door. I guess it took courage. After a while, I say to myself, "If you can't be friends with your friends, it's going to be worse yet dealing with your enemies."

Now every day after school, I go over to Stephanie's house. We do the things we used to do when we first met. We're closer now than ever. There's only one thing I wonder about. The other day, I started counting backward. Forget Drew and Mike. Could Tommy have been the father the second time Stephanie got pregnant?

proper respect

At this school, who runs things are the ones with the most props. "Props" means proper respect. You get that from having a gun, not backing down, and looking the right way. I understand that stuff, but I don't believe in it.

At first, everywhere I go, somebody be dissing me. I hear whispering, "Maybe Maurice is gay."

"No, he's a virgin."

Bobby, a friend of mine, starts singing "Welcome to the Virgin Islands" when I walk by.

I believe in abstinence. I'm not saying that you're not supposed to go out with anybody, still you've got to know how to have a little self-control.

I know there are a lot of people in my class who are virgins. But I can't say that to Bobby, or anyone else at school. I just ask, "Why are you saying that, Bobby?"

He says, "I'm dissing you to bring myself up. So that I can get friends."

I say, "You're bringing me down so you can get yourself up?"

"Right," he says. "Then I'll bring you up with me.

Whenever you get in a fight, whatever, I'll jump in. My brothers will jump in, too."

' "You're bringing me down so you can get yourself up?"

I don't want anybody to jump in for me. Then they might think I owe them. It's like gang stuff. It isn't brother stuff. I ignore Bobby and the others. But I don't get rid of their words. My brain records them, stores them, even though I don't want them there.

To deal with the dissing, I get down on my knees and pray to God. Christ went through things that I wouldn't even dream of going through. He had people spit on Him, call Him the worst of names, crucify Him. Without Him, I wouldn't be able to get through what I have in my life.

the competition

One day, along with the other students, I was coming late to performing arts class. Our teacher, Mrs. Mayedo, said, "Please, be quiet."

Half the students were giving her back chat, saying, "I ain't talking."

"You have to compete in a storytelling contest," she said. No one was paying much attention until she said, "You don't participate, you fail the class."

"What?" everybody said.

"There's a citywide storytelling contest," she said. "The first competition is here in school. Look for a story to memorize. It's best if it has a moral and promotes a message. The story must take ten minutes to tell. You have to stand still, your hands behind your back. You should smile and show poise. Have eye contact with the audience. Control how nervous or relaxed you appear. How you're dressed matters, too."

I thought I'd look for a story about why sex isn't good before marriage. But I couldn't find one. Mrs. Mayedo gave me a copy of *Mitchell's Folklore*. In it, I found an Italian folktale.

I took it home to memorize. That was not easy. I share a bedroom with my little brother. I began by sitting on my bed, saying it to myself.

My mum said, "Maurice, talking to yourself is not healthy."

I told her, "I'm doing this for a competition. If I don't do it, I'm going to fail my class." After that she encouraged me. I stood up and talked to the posters on my bedroom wall: Ice Cube, Shortie, Kid-Ice, The China-Man, Big Daddy King.

I was an American-born black with a Jamaican

mother telling an Italian folktale to pictures of rappers. My little brother said, "You be crazyman."

the winner

Everybody is supposed to memorize a story piece by piece. Otherwise you get a zero for the day. When Mrs. Mayedo calls some students' names, you hear, "I didn't memorize anything."

"I don't feel like doing it today."

"I forgot."

She calls on me. I've failed almost every class I've been in. I don't want to fail anymore. I get up and say a little piece. The other students have their tongues out their mouths. Their heads in their coats. Stretching. Yawning.

The second day Mrs. Mayedo says to us, "Go ahead, just tell me what you know."

They say, "I don't want to be in the competition."

"Tomorrow I'll be ready."

"I don't have it all together."

She calls on me. I keep at it. It's discouraging going up there. Still I learn the whole story in three days. It feels good. The only thing I have to do is get in the library for the school competition, and face the students.

I tell myself, "I've heard the other students. They're telling stories because they know they have to. They're not telling them because they like the story. I want to do it. I need to do it. And I'm going to beat every one of them."

But I don't want to go first. I say to Mrs. Mayedo, "Miss, please don't put me up first." I'm hoping they do it in alphabetical order, and they do. I get up there, and *brrrng,* the bell rings.

Mrs. Mayedo says, "You can compete tomorrow." I'm relieved. "And remember, Maurice, you have to keep still and keep your hands behind your back."

That night I practice with my hands buckled behind me. Standing straight. I know that the rules are strict on the length of the story. I time mine: nine minutes.

The next day I go to the library and tell my story. But, gosh, I get so into it that I start moving, sliding across the room, back and forth. I can't keep a smile off my face either. When I sit down afterwards, everybody's, like, wow. All the time in class, I wasn't that lively. But on the day of the contest when I got up in front of an audience, I was on.

The judges come back in the room and say, "The winner is . . . Maurice."

I'm, like, "I won? Yeah!"

I'm jumping, jumping. The students are into it, giving me five and everything. Mrs. Mayedo says, "This is the beginning. Next week is the district contest."

That night when I tell my mother, she's overjoyed. Later she makes me curried goat, my favorite. My little brother says, "Keep at it."

the setback

I'm sitting in class, doing work, and this kid brings me a message. Mrs. Mayedo has found out that the district contest is going on right then.

"Somebody made a mistake," she says. "No one told us when this next competition was."

I go to the office and say, "Can't somebody carry me in their car over to the contest?" They know what has happened, but nobody can help. There are all kinds of permissions and legal responsibility, and on and on. I say, "What do you mean you can't carry me? This is my moment in life."

I'm so angry; my mind is steaming. I get down on my knees and pray, "Nothing is impossible. In the Bible, God raised Lazarus from the dead. If God can do that, He can get me to have another chance."

I can hear Mrs. Mayedo on the phone. She's begging for me with the contest people. Finally they agree. "It is unfair. We'll tie him with the other person who won."

I'm really glad.

"Practice hard, Maurice," Mrs. Mayedo says.

When I leave the office, I run into Bobby. He says, "What're you smiling about?"

I tell him and he says, "That contest ain't black people's stuff. That's for white people. And worse yet, it's for girls."

"What are you talking about? It's nothing racial.

It's not just for girls. It's got to do with talent and ability."

I think, "With a friend like Bobby I don't need enemies."

"You look at Africa," I say. "Storytelling is an important part of tradition and the culture. In world history books, you see pictures of the village storyteller. He'd call all the village together, tell them how others go about certain things, and share their wisdom."

"Oh, please!" he says.

Bobby starts to walk away. Then he turns around and says, "Hey, man, break a leg."

"Thanks," I say, thinking maybe we can be friends after all. "I'm going to work to keep the devil out of my mind, go into the competition relaxed."

Bobby says, "Yeah, don't let your mind stray into worries whether some guy's gonna run into your house with a gun while you're gone."

the dream

The night before the citywide competition, I dream that I win and go to Washington. All the other states have to compete against me and I win.

In my dream I meet the President. I'm telling him my story, but it's a different story. It has to do with equalizing people. It's about men and women, eliminating prejudice, forgetting props, and being real friends.

That morning I'm ready. But I'm scared, too. My story is a little short. That length stuff bothers me. When I meet the other competitors, they're impressive.

I am the final person. I try to pick up last-minute tips. Some people are seated on a side that no one looks at. When I have my turn, I make sure I have eye contact with a lady in that corner.

I imagine that all the people in the audience are good friends of mine. They want me to feel comfortable. They don't want me to be so nervous I might get faint.

the best day

I felt good after the storytelling contest. I didn't have in my mind that I was going to win. When I heard one of the girls, I knew she stood out. The length of her story was just right. If it was close, they were going to go for the length.

I was right. That girl did win.

She told me later she'd done this contest three other times. She was born in Russia, and they have to memorize lots of stuff there.

When I came through the door at school, the classes were changing. I felt like everybody's eyes were on me.

I walked into performing arts class, and they were saying, "Did you win? Did you win? Did you win?"

I said, "Nah, second place." But they cheered for me. The principal came in, and they took Polaroid pictures of me with him and Mrs. Mayedo. They put them up in the library and the English office.

In gym class I still had on my white shirt and black pants from the contest. People were coming up, asking why I was dressed like that. They were kidding, "Did somebody die?"

"Were you recruited for the Jehovah's Witnesses?" The whole group that was with me started to laugh, but it was kind laughter. They weren't dissing me for looking or being different. They were proud of me.

Kids I didn't even know were saying, "You're the one from the storytelling competition?"

I'd say, "Yeah, that's me."

"Congratulations."

"Good for you."

Just then Bobby happened to walk by. I told him the contest results. "Was it a girl or a boy that won?" Bobby said.

"A girl."

"Was she black or white?"

"White."

"See, I told you. I knew it."

I said, "That doesn't have anything to do with it. She beat me for the right reasons. She had the longer story. Her voice control was good. Her eye contact was, too."

"Forget it," he said.

"I'll forget what you say, Bobby. And forgive you. You must be hurting inside."

He looked sad when I said that last part. I knew I was right. But still he shouldn't have tried to stand in the way of my success in the storytelling contest. That's not being any kind of friend.

The contest was such a nice experience.

The best day of my life; and next year I'll win.

Oh, boy, only thing better than that is salvation!

the smart one goes numb

It's Monday. I get a glass of apple juice, down thirty-two Sominex, then go and lay down. No note, nothing. About the only things I'm leaving are my messy room and my two-week overdue paper on Alice Walker.

Alice Walker is my favorite writer. As an African-American girl, I identify with her. But you know how you can get to a point when you like something so much that you can't explain it? That's how I feel. My words stay inside me, and it's driving me nuts.

Mrs. Voss, my teacher, is this wonderful woman who sometimes makes me nuts, too. Instead of getting angry at me for not having written the paper, she says, "Amelia, I'm sure whatever you come up with will be fine."

I want to shout at her, "I suck at writing!" But ever since I started school, I'm the smart one, the polite one, the go-getter. When I say, "I'm up a creek this time," the response is, "You'll figure something out. You always do."

Usually they're right. I'm a chameleon. If the people I'm with think I'm funny, I'm funny around them. If they think I'm deep and philosophical, I'm that way.

There are three people—Melissa, Arjeev, and Peggy—who I can be myself around. They're chameleons, too. With us Melissa is an opinionated extrovert. She was born to a teen mom who married for the first time only two years ago. Arjeev's from India, and is in the United States illegally. He's learned to be secretive. Peggy's parents pressure her to be perfect. She's also one of the most honest people I know.

With each other we put down the masks. Still it doesn't happen often enough. And not one person in my life is convinced my problems are real. They don't realize I'm having a breakdown. Suicide seems the only answer. I should know. I've had practice. This is my third attempt. It takes getting emotionally numb before I can go through with it. But Monday is really rotten.

Besides the English paper, I'm supposed to be chairperson of the arts festival. Then they switch and put in a guy who's less qualified. The difference is, he's a senior. I'm a junior. I'll have another chance.

They're, like, "Oh, it's no problem." Well, for me, it is.

On top of that, the UBS, United Black Students, say they're being denied the right to have an assembly. The principal says, "You don't have an agenda." There's rumor of a walkout.

Collin, a white guy from Honors English, yells at me, "Hey, ghetto girl, can't you minorities get your act together? What's the problem? I don't have people dropping college scholarship money on my doorstep. White males are the real minorities now."

"Fine," I say, "you think it's so great to be black, to be a minority. Accept the rest of it, the prejudice."

Meanwhile a black girl sees me talking to Collin, doesn't bother to find out the truth, and calls me a "wannabe white." I break down crying because I hate hatred. I don't know how to deal with it whatsoever.

suicide strategy

My plan was to swallow the Sominex and take an afternoon nap. That way they would be working while I was asleep. I wouldn't notice. Instead, I woke up about an hour later.

I had to use the bathroom, but it took me about two minutes just to get out of bed. I stood up and lunged toward the door. I pulled myself around the corner toward where the bathroom was.

My grandfather was there and I asked him, "Where's Mom?"

"Shopping for dinner," he said. Then he asked me, "Are you okay?"

"I'm sick," I said. "I'm going back to bed."

My mother got home a half an hour later. By that time I was scared. I tried to figure out how I could stay awake without letting them know that I was in trouble.

My little sister noticed that I was awake. My mom said, "Ask Amelia what she wants for dinner."

I tried to say, "I'm not hungry," but it came out garbled.

My mom said, "Come in here. I can't understand you."

I walked to the kitchen by hugging the wall.

"You look drunk," Mom said. "Your eyes are dilated."

My mouth could no longer form words.

She looked at me and said, "Amelia, what have you taken!"

"Nothing."

She grabbed me by the shoulders and said, "What have you taken?"

"Thirty-two Sominex."

"We're going to the hospital. Now!"

"I don't have any shoes on. Anyway, I'm fine."

I could hardly move. I could hardly form sentences. But I thought I was just going to walk into the kitchen, tell my mother, "I'm fine," then walk back into the bedroom and go to sleep.

At the hospital they said that my normal pulse rate was about ninety beats per minute. Right then mine had gotten down to twenty-five. If my mom hadn't found me for another half an hour, I could have had serious brain damage.

the roller coaster

When I'd been in the hospital four days, Melissa, Arjeev, and Peggy sent me roses and a card. There were other names on it, too. My first thought was, "Everybody cares!"

But when I read what they'd written, I was floored:

Dear Amelia,
    We love you. You're special. But if you're going to keep trying to kill yourself, we don't know if we can be there for you.
    Do we want to run the risk of having a friend who at any time could be gone? It's like dealing with some-one with a terminal illness. Maybe we want off the emotional roller coaster you've constructed.

Then all ten of them signed their names.

I'd been having literal nightmares about going to school and having everyone ignore me. I'd wake up cry-ing. But this card was more than I was prepared for.

I was trying to get myself ready, not only to deal with my family again, but to try to face those friends I most needed. Now they were saying they didn't know if they could be my friends anymore.

nobody's keeper

The first day back at school was hellish. The people I wasn't close to were glad to see me back, gave me hugs and all that. Melissa, Arjeev, and Peggy said practically nothing.

It was more, "We can't deal with this right now. You're on your own."

We'd known each other since elementary school. They'd been through my other attempts, too. My first was in seventh grade after my father had suddenly come back in my life. Before and after that he was never really there.

I was told that when I was about three months old, my parents got in a violent argument and he'd left town. He appeared for a week every couple years until I was about six. Then he disappeared until I was in seventh grade.

I think my mother still had feelings for him. But I told her, "I don't want to be around my dad."

She said, "Well, I think you need to."

I had such hatred for him. I felt if I saw him, I was going to kill him. Instead, I tried to kill myself. The second attempt came two years later for the usual reasons. Life got too much. And now this one.

By three P.M. that first day back, I had enough nervous energy to zoom around the two floors of our high school unable to stop. Mrs. Voss saw this and grabbed me.

She said, "Amelia, you've had time to think about what you did and how you might like your friends to respond. You've got to give your friends time to process all this."

She was right. The next day at school I said to them, "Look, this is the best I can do. I'll give you a week to say anything you have to say. If you're mad, tell me. If you want to lecture me, do it."

Arjeev gave me the how-selfish-suicide-is response.

Peggy said, "You're such a great friend."

Melissa said, "You have so much to live for. You always give me good advice. How dare you try to take yourself away from us."

No one asked, "Why did you do it?" And it was ironic, every reason they gave me to live was something that made them feel good. I was ready to scream, "How dare you ask me to live just because I make your life richer. I'm miserable." At the same time, I knew it was hard for them. I had put them through a lot.

The three of them seemed to be expecting an apology, which made me upset. Melissa and Arjeev love to party. They get drunk. They drive. They've all slept around a little and, you know, that's supposed to be cool.

Those are all the things that could end their lives or at least change how they live it. They could die in a car crash. They could become a parent at sixteen.

But they don't apologize to me for running the risk of those things happening. Sometimes they even think it's pretty funny. They laugh about their behavior.

The truth was I didn't feel like saying I was sorry or making up excuses.

Arjeev and Melissa started to pretend it didn't happen. Only Peggy wanted to talk. When we met in library study hall, she told me, "I'm trying to get to the point where I'm self-sufficient. To never have anyone or anything that I cannot live without. I really can't be there to support you or to bail you out. I can't give you encouraging words."

I was starting to feel mad. "Peggy, I'm not asking for your pity or your sympathy," I said.

"I know you're not. But I just thought you should know I can't be your keeper."

"But I never asked you to."

She said, "Whether you kill yourself is up to you. I can't afford to care."

"Don't worry," I said. "I'll only care about people who are dead. They're safe." After that conversation, I was glad Arjeev and Melissa didn't want to discuss my suicide attempt.

senior goal

I'm a senior now. My goal is to get through this year without ending up in the hospital.

I'm in counseling. My therapist tells me that trying to numb myself to people is not healthy. She also points out that whenever I'm hurting, I tell people I'm fine and hope they won't notice.

She says I'm a good actress, only most of my acting isn't on stage. It's in life. I'm supposed to try to be more honest with my friends. As far as saying, I can't do it. Instead of taking everything on, trying to be superwoman.

I'm trying to be more open, to where they don't have the excuse, "We didn't know you were hurting." I'm probably doing less lying in trying to evaluate my-self.

I'm finding more things that are funny. I'm not always depressed. Of course, like most people, I'm not always happy, either.

"What's the shrink think?" Melissa asks.

"She's hinted that I'm manic depressive. I'm on Prozac now."

Arjeev says, "Do you think it's helping?"

"I don't know," I say.

Melissa says, "Have you thought about killing yourself?"

"No," I say, "but the majority of the time—ninety-nine percent—I was never thinking about killing myself." I mean, it's like asking an alcoholic, "Are you ever going to take a drink again?"

> " "Whether you kill yourself is up to you. I can't afford to care.""

I don't spend much time with Peggy anymore. But Arjeev has become an even better friend. I tell him, "Sometimes I'm scared. But, I know, too, that I have a lot of love to give."

"Why do you think you were put on earth?" he asks.

"I don't know. I don't think I was meant to be here to

do anything in particular. Like maybe I won't become president or be nominated homecoming queen. But years later, you'll go, 'Wow, there was a girl in high school who could make me stop and think.' "

Not to be bragging, but I have some value.

What do you think?

"You can't ask friends to go farther than they're willing to go. They can't be your therapist."
— student, Locust Valley Junior-Senior High School, Locust Valley, New York

"Amelia should find friends who are more understanding. She should also take time out and review her problems in her mind. She should be her own friend and not be afraid of who she is."
— student, Lawrence Middle School, Lawrence, New York

"I think Amelia's stuck in what we call a 'distress pattern,' a rigid form of behavior. She can't see outside

it very well. Something makes her believe suicide is her best alternative.

"She could spend time in counseling sessions realizing that whatever is making her attempt suicide happened a long time ago and is not reality now. If she wants to go back and cry about whatever happened, she can do that. But her life is too valuable to be wasting much time still doing that.

"She's a wonderful person who should focus on noticing how many friends she has and how well loved she really is."

—Jenny Sazama, International Reference Person for Young Adults in Co-Counseling, Teen Empowerment, South End, Boston

ayeisha, bill, and catherine

tension and gossip

I pledge allegiance to the flag of the
United States of America and to the Re-
public for which it stands; one na-
tion, under God, indivisible, with
liberty and justice for all.

*This is an interview with California high school
students Ayeisha, Bill, and Catherine.*

Ayeisha: The uproar started in class one day. Some guy's
sitting at his desk during the pledge. Another guy says to
him, "You can get a free lunch ticket, but you can't stand
and say the pledge."

I hadn't stood for the pledge for six years. It wasn't
anything new to me or a lot of students. But this time
some teachers went to Mr. Gingel, the principal. They
were worried it might turn into a problem. So for the next

three days, the pledge wasn't part of the morning intercom announcements.

Bill: Everybody's in a daze first period, anyway. When the pledge wasn't recited, I sort of thought, "Gee, that's funny." But beyond that, I knew lots of kids didn't stand because they felt they had the right not to stand. Then some kids just didn't care. What? Me stand?

Nobody missed the pledge until that Sunday when an article came out in the city newspaper. You know how the media likes to stick things in to make a good story? This headline said, CENTRAL STOPS SAYING THE PLEDGE.

Catherine: I'm the teen reporter for the paper. I broke the story. Mr. Gingel had told me, "Some people are making racist statements against those who aren't standing. I want to suspend the pledge while we figure out a way to have students air their grievances."

I thought, "This'll make a good article. I'll report the facts without taking a position."

The next day my editor called me up in the middle of school. "I want to move this story from the youth desk to the news desk," he said. "I'm assigning a reporter to cover the issue. You'll be mentioned at the end as 'teen correspondent.'"

I was excited. I had no idea it would be front-page news.

Bill: That Monday there were reporters from other papers, the AP wire service, even TV crews. Everybody was in a turmoil. It was getting blown out of proportion and turned into a racial thing. It wasn't that way.

Before all this I never thought about looking around to see who was standing. That day as we were saying the pledge, I started doing that. My friends did, too.

In the cafeteria it was all tension and gossip, "Hey, in my class so-and-so didn't stand." There's always been, like, this definite racist undercurrent. Derogatory words about "all these #$%@* white people are in my way." And "there're too many $@*# black people at this school."

The trouble over standing for the pledge brought these feelings to the surface.

Ayeisha: What we read in the paper made it sound like black students at Central don't do this and don't do that.

Media people started coming around asking everyone, "Is it true?"

"A lot of people, black and white, don't say the pledge," I said.

I felt pressure. Everybody knows me at school. I'm a class officer, editor of the literary magazine, in the drama club. And I'm black. From Day One I'd made a conscious decision I would be with everybody, not just with black students. But I am president of the African-American Union.

That Monday it was, like, I was supposed to be representing everybody brown in the school. It was intimidating. I'd say to myself, "Now, Ayeisha, think before you speak, clarify what you want to say, and back it up with some kind of paperwork."

I pulled quotes from Edgar Allan Poe to Malcolm X.

I said to the other students, "Tell the media how you feel. You're not wrong for what you feel."

Catherine: It was weird at school. Some kids gave me dirty looks. They resented the media attention. My friends joked that I was a "troublemaker." But really they were proud I'd gotten a story on the front page. They were supportive, even later when they didn't agree with me.

Bill: I know everybody at least in the senior class. I have about twenty good friends. They see me as honest and outspoken. One time I ended up balanced on top of this kid's car, reading a speech about the unfairness of a curfew.

I guess you could say my friends look up to me. That's a responsibility. All my close friends are white, but I don't feel I should segregate myself. It's interesting to get in with people of different cultures and colors.

With the flag thing, I thought if you didn't want to say the pledge, you should have told Mr. Gingel, "I don't like people aggravating me for not standing." He shouldn't have discontinued the pledge 'cause someone had a problem with it.

the forum

Catherine: Mr. Gingel decides we should have a student-run forum in the auditorium. We can say what we want on the issue.

The first question is, "Why don't you stand?"

A black student says, "Our ancestors were brought here from another country. We didn't ask to be here. I'd be a hypocrite if I stood. I don't feel I'm free."

Bill: I say, "What do you mean you're not free? You have as many rights and opportunities as white people. Sometimes more."

Ayeisha: I say, "As an African-American I can't go into a single store at the Green Point Mall without being watched. I go to a restaurant, and they serve white people before they serve me."

Catherine: A voice at the back of the room yells, "So go to another restaurant."

Ayeisha: I blow up. I say, "As long as my money is green, just like yours, you must serve me." But it's more than that. Take the time I was learning to drive. I was in my parents' car, a New Yorker. An officer pulled me over, assuming either I had stolen it or was selling drugs. Now, where were my "rights and opportunities" to drive the family car without being hassled?

Catherine: Some student interrupts Ayeisha and says, "Yeah, yeah, but look at something like medical school.

You can rank lower on the tests than I do and get in. Anyway, you were born American. You are American. You shouldn't have any excuse."

Ayeisha: I say, "Excuse about what? I love the country, but I've already told you how the country loves me back. I want it to be better. I want 'liberty and justice for all' to apply to me, and to homeless people, to starving people. . . . And I want someone to explain to me why I can't pray to God in school, but I'm supposed to pledge to Him?"

Catherine: I don't know how to answer that. Instead, I tell the forum a little something I learned researching the pledge.

I say, "When the pledge was first written, it said 'my' flag, not 'the' flag. Then they changed it so people wouldn't feel, 'Hey, this is not my flag.' By saying 'the' flag it would accommodate people from other cultures."

Bill: Okay, but I still think whether you stand is a personal issue. People have died for that flag. I'm not pledging the government. I'm pledging for my belief in the country's future, not for its past. I'm proud of my country.

A black student says stuff, like, "Fine, but what do you know about my African culture?"

I say, "I'm not in Africa. I'm in America. I learn about American culture. My grandparents are from Italy. I don't go around saying, 'Hey, what do you know about Italian culture?' I learn about it, but I don't expect other people to. And you shouldn't expect me to learn about African culture.

"The United States is never going to be a perfect country. But we have to strive for what we can, and sitting down for the flag is not going to make it any better."

Ayeisha: In sixth grade I made a decision not to stand. As punishment I got detention. After that I stood up. I needed school more than I needed detention.

In seventh grade I told my teacher, "I don't believe in the wording."

She left me alone because I wasn't disrespecting anybody else when the pledge came on. In ninth grade my teacher had a problem with it again.

I went to him after class and said, "I had two uncles and three cousins in the Gulf War. I felt very strongly that I wanted them back home. I wanted that whole war thing over. But saying the pledge was not my way to have that happen. If you feel I'm disrespecting you, I'll sit in the back of the class so you don't see me."

Most of us were taught the pledge of allegiance in the first grade. We didn't know what we were reciting then, and we still don't now. We just say it, mechanically. I feel, if this is patriotism, I don't need it.

I respect your right to stand up. You should respect my right to sit down.

Catherine: I'm beginning to think the more we say it's not a racial issue, the more it seems it is. That's counterproductive. And we aren't discussing the issue when it comes down to, "I don't have to stand." "You should."

I have my own compromise. I stand, but I don't say the pledge. I love this country. I have respect for it and the people around me. I wouldn't want to live anywhere else.

But starting in tenth grade, I realized I was saying the pledge as I was doing my homework. I had no idea the history of the pledge. All we're made to do is memorize it.

I think I can be patriotic in other ways. I speak at school board meetings. I help clean up the Veterans' Cemetery for Memorial Day. That's how I show my feelings for my country.

This forum shouldn't be about whether we're for or against the pledge. It's whether we think it should be required.

A girl I've known since fifth grade says, "Well, Catherine, maybe your parents don't teach you patriotism at home. Mine do."

I'm, like, "Excuse me!"

A guy says, "I think that anybody who can't stand for the pledge is a bastard."

I say, "Well, I guess I'll just have to be a bastard."

Ayeisha: When the newspaper got into this issue, the parents got into it. They read the article and it was, like, "Oh, it's black and white." Kids brought their parents' attitudes to school.

We can't teach parents to stop hating people who are

a different race. They're old dogs; they won't learn new tricks. We're new puppies. We are supposed to be open. We can learn whatever we want to learn. Let's not carry the reflection of racism to school.

Bill: Racism is not helping anybody, anywhere. We talk about how to stop it. There are suggestions like we could get T-shirts and posters with the word "racism" in a circle with a slash through it.

Students, especially popular ones, would wear them. The attitude would be, "Racism isn't good." Someone says, "Let's have breakfasts where kids from different races invite each other."

We schedule a series of meetings to talk about these things. Tempers begin to cool, but suddenly we hear a voice say, "You don't like this country? Leave! We won't miss you."

the fallout

Catherine: At first we were happy to have a forum because they gave us soda and donuts and we got out of class. By the end we were still stuck on differences of opinion.

I think, though, the newspaper article catalyzed the issue. Without the media attention we wouldn't have discussed patriotism and racism in the same way. Everybody should be admired for speaking their mind.

Now at our school the issue's more about respecting your peers.

Bill: The pledge is being said again. Some stand; some don't. More blacks don't stand, but it's not just blacks. It never was.

I learned that you have to respect other people's opinions even if you think it's not right. I always thought that standing for the pledge was my patriotic boost for the day. Some people don't think that.

It's not that they're bad people. They just have a different opinion.

Ayeisha: The flag crisis tore me down. I was so tired and emotionally drained, I got sick. When my grades fell, I thought, "I let myself down. I'm going nowhere."

I wished I could have made it clear it was just the students expressing their minds about the country in which they are living. About how they want to make it better.

And I wished one day I would be able to stand up, say the pledge, and mean it. We should be striving for the pledge to live up to its words.

david

real life
virtual
love

I'm not a recluse. I hang out with friends at school. But since I was eight, I've been calling computer bulletin boards. My favorites are multiline. I can just sit at home and type back and forth with eight to sixteen people.

During the school year, I spend about two hours a day on them. During the summers, it's all day. I turn the computer on, go into my communications program . . . hear my modem change from a ring to a high-pitched sound as it connects.

I'm in.

There's a welcome message. I log in. I type in either my alias or my real name, depending on what kind of bulletin board it is. I think a lot about my aliases. When I was a kid, I'd pick comic book characters. Then TV characters. Now I usually make up something with a science fiction feel, like Trexxon.

My friends at school come over. They don't consider me a nerd or hacker with glasses. Instead, they want me to show them the bulletin boards. They say, "You do all this?" They all want computers with modems, too.

I can't explain to them what happens inside me when I'm at my computer. Boards get me in a mood. I go into another world. On boards people can become someone else. They can pretend to be older. They can get into role-playing.

They can be who they are without scaring people. That's important to me, too. In real life, people don't see me, or anybody. They see their weird prejudices. Like, now I'm sixteen, I look older. I'm six feet tall and weigh two hundred pounds. I have long hair in a ponytail and wear a jeans jacket. If you see me without knowing me, I look kind of like a threatening jock.

Over the computer, they know me. They know how I am. I make good friends without ever meeting F2F, face-to-face. Mainly, though, boards are a lot of guys. I'd guess it's a thirty-two to one ratio, male to female. And that's being generous. See, what happens is this. Once females get on, it's open season. The younger guys, especially, badger them over and over, **What's your name? What's your number?** The unwritten rule is, "Try to date them."

I never thought that would apply to me.

chat mode

It was a Saturday, June third. I was in a good mood, sitting at my computer, talking to the regular people on teleconference. On the screen appears this message: **Hi, everybody. My name's Michelle. How are you guys doing?**

I typed **Hello** back. Someone typed a message about a recent movie. Other people were saying what they thought of it. While everybody else was talking, I looked up Michelle on the registry. That's, like, a bio you can fill out if you want to when you're a new user. You can put in your real name, not just your computer name, your hair and eye color, marital status, favorite food, favorite pastime. You can also leave a brief summary line.

Michelle's line said, **Howdy, pardner. Smile. I'm twenty-eight.**

I was five when she graduated from high school.

I thought, "Oh, well, maybe we could become friends."

There's a thing called a chat mode where you and whoever accepts your "chat" can type to each other and no one else can see or read it. It's a private thing.

On Michelle's monitor it said, **Trexxon is requesting a chat with you. Will you accept?**

On my monitor I saw these words, **Sure, but how old are you?** That was her first question.

I typed, **How old do you want me to be?**

She said, **The age you are.**

I was honest with her. I said, I'm sixteen.

Do you know how old I am?

Yeah, you're twenty-eight. We can still be friends, can't we?

She said, There's no problem about our ages.

I saw on your bio that you live in New Jersey, but you go to a church in Missouri. I'm confused.

I'm at my parents' house in Hackensack for six weeks this summer. I go to school in Missouri.

In the past six months, I'd started to go to parties with people I met over the boards. I said, Maybe, we could meet? What's your number?

You're limited to an hour on this board, and my time was running out. She said, I don't know about that. I've been told not to give out my number.

They always tell female users, "You don't know who's out there."

I said again, How about you call me? and I typed out my number. Just then I got kicked off; my hour was up. I thought, "Oh, no, what if she doesn't call!" I waited and waited for my phone to ring.

And then it did.

Michelle.

She sounded different. She didn't act her age. She kind of acted like me. I wanted to meet her right away. I didn't know hardly anything about her, except I knew I wanted to see her. I'd never met a woman this way before. I'd never really dated a lot.

I said, "What about meeting tomorrow? In person?"

She said, "I have to work, but I'm free next Saturday.

First, though, do you have a picture of yourself? I want to see what you look like before you come over."

"Will you send me one of you?"

She said she would, but she didn't. I put mine in the mail right away.

F2F

That week I'm getting excited, anxious, butterflies, the whole thing. I don't tell anybody what I'm going through. I don't talk to my friends at school. I don't even bring it up on the bulletin board.

I never meet anyone just one-on-one. Always before I met someone new in a group. This is going to be me and Michelle. Alone.

I say to my dad, "Can you drive me to a friend's house?"

He says, "Which friend?"

"My friend Michelle."

"David, you don't have a friend Michelle."

"I do now."

He uses the bribery trick, "Okay, as long as you clean your room." I do that and then we leave. She only lives about twenty minutes away.

It's noon and I knock on the door. No one answers. What if she doesn't like what I look like in the photo and now pretends she's not home?

Finally I hear "Come on in." Her parents have this

split-level house. I can see she's on the phone down the steps. "Go sit down," she says, "till I finish talking."

She hangs up and says, "That was my friend Ruben. He runs a bulletin board. He's having a picnic. I have to go to work at three-thirty, but we could go for a while."

"Okay," I say. She picks up her car keys and we're out the door. "What will we be doing there?" I ask.

"There's going to be food, talking, and volleyball," she says.

"Wow, I love volleyball."

"Me, too."

Michelle comes up to my nose. I feel comfortable around her. At the picnic we talk about Ruben and his wife, this bad relationship that Michelle's trying to get over, and how both of us play chess.

A woman named Brenda comes up, and Michelle says, "How old do you think David is?"

"Twenty-three?" she says. Michelle and I look at each other and laugh. Then all of a sudden it's time for her to go. She gives me this long hug and says, "I'll try to call you tonight when I have a break at work."

F2F+

At home that night we had pizza. I kept wondering whether she'd call. I decided to convince myself she wouldn't. I didn't want to get my hopes up. Around eleven-thirty I was watching some TV when the phone rang.

Michelle said, "Can I come over?"

Wow!

I live with my mother and my father. She wanted to come over at midnight.

"Yeah, sure," I told her. "I'll sneak you in the basement."

I build science fiction models down there. My parents know I can do that for hours. My mother was still up. When she said, "What are you doing?" I had my excuse ready.

"I'm going to work on my models," I said.

Michelle had said she'd get to my house around twelve-fifteen. When it was approaching that time, I snuck out the back, ran around the house, and into the front. There she was, getting out of her car.

"How are you doing?" she said.

"Oh, I'm fine," I said.

"David, why are we going through the basement?"

"My parents are home," I said.

"I forgot."

There's not much furniture in the basement. Just the desk where I work and two chairs. We started talking, but we had to be quiet doing that. Then I heard some noise upstairs. I went up to see who it was.

It was my mother! I said, "Hey, Mom, how come you're not asleep?"

She said, "It's so hot I wanted a glass of lemonade."

I couldn't believe she picked that moment to be

thirsty. I went back to the basement and I could see Michelle was nervous now. Her arms and legs were shaking. I tried not to show how nervous I was.

We both calmed down as we started to open up to each other. She noticed a scar I had on my leg. I told her how I fell off a motorcycle when I was ten.

She said, "I'm very insecure about my body."

"There's nothing wrong with it," I said.

"Well, I'm flat-chested."

She was concerned I wouldn't like her because of that. I told her, "That doesn't bother me. That's not where your brains are." She liked that. She was making me feel I could express my emotions.

I have an old black-and-white TV in the basement. I found this mattress I forgot was down there, too. We lay down, just talking and watching TV. We fell asleep. Around four in the morning, she said, "It's getting to be dawn soon. I should leave. I have to work tomorrow."

We were both groggy. But I didn't want my parents to come down and find us. They'd ground me until I was eighty-three. "Are you going to call me?" I said as I walked her to her car.

She promised she would. And she did.

computer games

When Michelle calls, we talk about how much we're missing each other, even though we've just been together. I'm really happy. She's my first official possible girlfriend.

I tell my friends at school about her. When they want to know her age, I say, "She's nineteen." I worry they might say, "She's robbing the cradle." Or, "David, she's leading you astray."

For the next five weeks, school's out, and Michelle and I are together every day. I don't have time for the bulletin boards. My school friends are either away or busy. All my time is consumed by Michelle.

We talk about marriage. I say, "What if I proposed on the bulletin board?"

"I'd kill you," she says. "There's only one way you could do it that's really romantic. That's at a prom."

The weekend my parents are gone, Michelle comes over. We spend eight hours together. In the early evening, my grandmother stops by to check on me.

She calls and tells my parents, "A girl's there." They make me get on the phone.

My alibi is Michelle wanted to borrow a computer

> My alibi is Michelle wanted to borrow a computer game.

game. "Why was she waiting in your bedroom?" my father asks.

"She had to wait somewhere," I say.

"When we get back there's going to be hell to pay."

Since I'm already in trouble, Michelle doesn't leave until two in the morning after putting some vodka in my Mountain Dew.

INTERNET rescue

On August first, Michelle leaves to go back to Missouri for school. The day before, she gives me this little necklace. It has a heart that's in half. She has one half and I have the other.

We go to the movies. I take her out to Red Lobster for dinner. I feel numb. I start thinking about proposing to her. I'd help with the prom and get the principal to let me up on stage. Before the last dance, I'd tell people not to drink and drive home. "Everybody bow your heads in a moment of si-

> "Why was she waiting in your bed-room?" my father asks.

lence," I'd say, and I'd pull out the ring and ask her right there.

I think she'd like that.

Morgan and Elizabeth, two of my friends from school, are back from vacations. I show them Michelle's picture. "I wrote her poetry," I say.

Elizabeth says, "I want to meet her." She can't believe I can be romantic. When I tell her Michelle and I want to get married, she says, "Do you think maybe you've jumped to the end of the relationship before having all the things in the middle?"

I don't want to listen. I go home and turn on my computer. I hear the high-pitch sound as the modem connects. The welcome message. I log in.

One guy who calls his board Board Zilla says, **Where were you?**

A message from Lock Out comes on, **Trexxon, we were worried. Are you okay?**

A guy who calls himself Python says, **I thought you were gone and buried.** There are all these people saying the same thing, they thought I'd died. I'd been a regular caller and then suddenly I'd disappeared. At that moment, I know the truth. I feel closer to some of the people on the boards than to the kids at school.

I can talk to them more easily. I can say things that I can't say to people where I have to look them in the eye. I just type my feelings. They don't know my school friends, so they can't talk about me behind my back.

I say, **I've been with my girlfriend.**
Who is it?

Her name's Michelle. Maybe you remember see-ing her on here. They do. I feel lonely now that she's gone, I say.

My screen lights up with all these messages. My friends are comforting me. Trexxon, apply for account #s from INTERNET, where universities are networked through the modem.

Anybody can apply. You don't have to be in col-lege.

In two weeks you'll get your passwords. Then pick a time to both be on INTERNET and let the ro-mance continue.

I say, Thanks a lot. That's a great idea.

I'm at my computer. There on my screen is Michelle's first message: I'm lonely for you! I was sick last week and wished you were here to take care of me.

It's frustrating. We can't even hold hands, I type back.

This is what I'll do when I see you at Christmas: xxxooooxoxoxoxoxooooooxoxxxoooooooooooooooxoxo xoxoxoxooooxoxoxoxo.

elena

the fight

A best friend is someone who likes you for what you are inside your heart, not what you look like.

I first met Polly when we were in fifth grade. I talked to her a lot, and after a while I took her places with me, too. One day at school, they came and got me from my classroom. Polly was sick. Would I come talk to her until her mom could get here?

I said, "Sure."

I lay down on a mat next to her. "Hi, Polly," I said. "How are you feeling?" She looked up at me and smiled a big smile. She knew I wanted to be her friend. And that was her way of letting me know that she wanted to be mine.

See, when Polly was two years old, a baby aspirin lodged in her throat. She went into a coma normal and came out with cerebral palsy, seizures, and diabetes. She had to use a wheelchair. She spoke through her facial expressions.

Before Polly, I didn't know anyone with a disability. They were in a special ed trailer back of school. Then regular students were asked if we wanted to go in and read to them, play together on the computer, go to lunch with them. I was one of the people who did it.

In sixth grade I said to my teacher, "Can Polly come into our classroom for an hour or two? I'd read to her and stuff." He checked with the other teachers and said, "Okay."

Me and Polly gave each other attention. I began to tell her things I didn't tell other people. I joked that my secrets were safe with her. She couldn't talk.

Polly let me know the other side of the picture. In her own way she said, when you have a disability, the way you act is the way you're going to be treated.

When I looked at her, I didn't see the wheelchair. I saw her.

a life

More of our friends started getting involved with Polly, too. We became, like, a big, old group. Polly would come over to our houses to hang out, listen to the radio, spend the night. She let us know she was glad we helped her have a life.

In seventh grade some regular students said they didn't want to eat in the same lunchroom with kids with disabilities. We told them they were wrong. They didn't listen. I don't get mad when people don't seem to understand. I try to explain.

"Let's make up a disability story and videotape it," I said.

The story had these kids with snotty attitudes toward kids with disabilities. Then one day they got in a car accident and ended up in wheelchairs. You never know about tomorrow.

We were getting ready to graduate and go off to Lincoln High School, when I said to an administrator, "Polly's going to be able to come with us, isn't she?"

"No," the administrator said. "Lincoln can't provide for all Polly's special needs. She'll go to Washington High."

"It's a thirty-minute bus ride to a school where she doesn't know anybody," I said. "She lives two blocks from Lincoln."

The administrator wasn't listening.

plans

People say I'm mature. I can think as an adult. I believe, "Stay young in the heart, but smart in the mind."

I say to our group, "They can't just tear somebody away from a great friendship. Remember what we learned this year about the Constitution. We have the right to protest the government's mistakes."

A girl, Luz, says, "Right. They can't discriminate against a person because of a handicap."

Someone else says, "Let's make a petition and have everybody sign it." We give the five hundred signatures to the high school district. The special ed people are impressed with what we feel, but they say they know best.

We have another meeting where we decide to picket the high school district office. Fifty kids show up with signs. To raise money we make and sell a video about our battle. We write rap songs. We stand outside an evaluation meeting for Polly trying to talk to the special ed people.

> " "We're all different and alike," I say.

Our friend Claire tells them, "In your time you segregated handicapped kids in one handicapped program. We think, treat them as regular people."

"We're all different and alike," I say. "Polly's white. I'm a Mexican-American. Polly's in a wheelchair. I walk. But we're the same inside."

Luz starts to say, "We'll hire a nurse—" when they interrupt her to say, "No."

Our group is close even before we start fighting for Polly. This helps us get closer. Still sometimes we get mad at each other. Polly, too. Well, mostly she gets mad at me.

It's because of a guy. He wants a lot of my time. If I'm with Polly, he's jealous. If I'm with him, I hurt her. I try to spend time with both of them. He's important to me, but I say to her, "I'll never let a guy come between you and me. They're not worth it."

a future

A school year has come and gone with Polly at the other school. Me and Polly, Luz, Claire, Frank—fourteen of us start to go to conferences all over the state to tell our story.

We meet Diane Lipton, a lawyer with something called Disability Rights Education and Defense Fund, DREDF. She says, "I'll file a lawsuit against the high school district."

We all feel excited, but I feel stressed, too. I'm pregnant. The doctor's worried I'll have my baby early. "Stay in bed for this last month," he tells me. I remember the day Polly was sick at school and I had been there for her. Now it's reversed. She keeps me company.

Meanwhile, the lawsuit heats up. The school dis-

> "Polly's white. I'm a Mexican-American. Polly's in a wheelchair. I walk."

trict tells the lawyer Polly's mom bribed us to be her daughter's friend! The lawyer says, "See you in court."

Just before the trial starts, the lawyers sit down to eight hours of mediation to try to settle the case. And they do. We win! Starting in fall, Polly will be in school with us. We pick her up in a stretch limo for a press conference at Lincoln High.

We have such a celebration.

camille

friendly
betrayal

I'm in ninth grade now. For K through seven, I went to private school. I had one main friend, Debbie. Debbie and I would be in and out of each other's house. I knew her mother and father; she knew mine.

We were family.

We both liked "Big Lizard in My Backyard" by the Dead Milkmen. We were bachelorettes together. And we were both antidrug. There was drug education at school. "You know, drugs are so stupid," Debbie'd say. "Why would anyone want to use them?"

I was what they call alternative. Those are the people who have opinions and speak them. They listen to music that's happy. Hardly any of it is about love.

Debbie and I agreed, we didn't want to be shallow like the popular people.

putting up with put-downs

In eighth grade, Debbie and I both transferred out to the same public school. After a few weeks it hit me. The drive to be with the popular kids was like a contagious disease. It was spreading to Debbie.

She'd say, "If anybody asks you if you've heard some song, just say you like it, even if you've never listened to it. That'll make you sound cool."

Once when I didn't have name-brand pants on, I heard, "Ewww, Camille, did you buy those at Stop 'n Save?"

"Why are you ranking on me?" I said to her. She walked away.

A girl I'd just met named Shannon overheard what we said. "You shouldn't let her put you down," she said. "Being different sets you apart from others. You need friends around when you're doing something wrong. If you get caught, they help share the blame and cover for you."

conforming to society

Shannon moved away for nine months; her divorced parents had shared custody.

Then Debbie met Lyle. Lyle was a headbanger. Here

headbangers listen to Metallica. They have an attitude, like, they rule and you better not get in their way.

Debbie got into the deal of dressing black.

All she would talk about was Lyle, Lyle, Lyle. It was obnoxious. I started to get annoyed with her. We had had the best relationship. And now, since we never saw each other, we couldn't even discuss it. She'd disappeared into Lyle.

I heard a rumor Lyle was a drug dealer.

The next thing I knew, she slept with him. When I saw her, I said, "Debbie, I don't want to hear your personal business. So what if I'm a virgin."

I felt lonely. I didn't have any main friend other than her. I thought, "Maybe I need a boyfriend."

There was this guy, Brian. Whenever he smiled at me, I was, like, "Oh, he smiled at me." He was a friend of Lyle's, and a headbanger, too.

I wanted to be their friend and stuff. I think everybody conforms to society at one time or another. Debbie and Lyle and Brian and I started to hang out together.

I've had a curiosity with the night, things that go unexplained. I began dressing dark. I wore heavy, black eyeliner. I looked dangerous. I've always liked to have people the tiniest bit afraid of me.

breaking free

I went out with Brian for five months and three days. I barely did anything with him. I don't think I even liked him, which kind of disgusted me.

So I called him up and said, "I can't go out with you anymore. It's not right."

"I don't need this," he said, and hung up.

When I started crying, Debbie said, "It's okay," before she went off on Lyle.

Being broken up was a load lifted off my shoulders. I became more individualistic and more creative. People were coming up to me, saying, "Wow, you changed from dark night to great day."

Still I needed somebody to help me with the pain of Debbie not being around. And right then Shannon moved back. She started becoming my support. When I thought about dying my hair, when I mismatched my clothes, she said, "You look neato-burrito."

Shannon and I could talk to each other without any fear of having negative things come of it. Debbie would lie about things. She'd become a poser, dressing to get attention.

Shannon wasn't afraid to give her opinion. Once when we talked about drugs, she said, "I'm dead set against them, especially acid. You can have flashbacks."

confronting debbie

Debbie and I share a locker. One morning she says to me, "Camille, I bought some pot."

"What!" I say. "We're antidrug people."

"You mean you're not curious? I think I'm going to buy some acid today."

"Debbie," I say, "don't do that. You could have a bad trip."

"Oh, you can create your mood."

"Who did you hear that from?"

"That's what Lyle says."

"Great. He was probably drunk or stoned at the time."

After Debbie leaves, I think about what she said. I'm seriously worried about her. That night I tell my mom about it. "Do you want me to call Debbie's parents?" she asks.

I say, "No, don't do that. She'll hate me forever."

I think some more and then call Shannon. I say, "Maybe we should talk to Debbie."

"She's stubborn," Shannon says.

"Right. She'll deny everything. What about talking to her parents instead?"

"She'll probably go out and tell all her friends," says Shannon. "She'll be mad and they'll hate us."

"If we tell Debbie's mother, she'd kill herself right there. But her dad is more experienced. What's important is that none of us wants her OD'd."

"Okay," Shannon says, "you call."

I go through the biggest stress scene dialing Debbie's number. We decide, if she picks up the phone, I'll hang up. I don't want Debbie to know I'm confronting her.

The phone rings three times, then Mr. Gruen picks up and says "Hello."

I say, "Hey, Mr. Gruen, how are you guys? I don't want you to freak out about this or anything. We're doing this because we love Debbie. We think she could get hurt. She bought some pot. And she told me earlier today that she was going to buy acid."

I hear his gasp. He keeps repeating, "Ohmigod, ohmigod."

"I'm sorry I had to be the one to tell you this." I'm wondering what he's going to do. I'm kind of scared.

"You never believe this can actually happen to your child," he finally says. I feel I'm getting ready to cry, because of the emotion of his words.

"How do you know about this?" he says.

I tell him all that she has said. He says, "Thank you so much for calling."

finding a solution

The next morning at school Debbie comes storming up to me at our locker. "So last night we had a family meeting, Camille. My dad accused me of being a drug addict. I said, 'What are you talking about?' and he said, Camille called and said that she and Shannon knew for a fact that I was definitely using pot and acid."

"That's not what I said. I told him, 'We know you bought some pot and acid, but we had no solid proof that you're using them.' "

"I told my dad the same thing. And that I flushed it. I flushed it. But he didn't believe me. He believed you."

I don't say anything.

"Oh," she says, "and thanks for telling my dad and my family first. How tacky."

"We're just saving your life, Debbie. Appreciate it." We walk into class with this major silence between us.

I remember once Debbie said how bad my hair was. During the coming days it's like ten times worse than that. She tells Lyle all about it. He calls me up and says, "Camille, why are you saying this stuff about Debbie?"

I say, "Excuse me. I don't want to talk to you. You have a problem, go to Debbie."

Shannon and I are sort of frustrated. We know that Mrs. Gruen likes to ignore things that are bad. We think she will deny what we have said about Debbie. She'll think, "This cannot happen to my sweet little daughter. Shannon and Camille are just making it up."

We are convinced she'll talk Mr. Gruen into forgetting about it. He loves her so much. But he doesn't give in. They have Debbie drug-tested.

We are in drama class when she passes me this note: "I want to have a talk with both of you." After class, the three of us meet, Shannon, me, and Debbie.

She says, "First, I want you to know the drug test was negative."

"Well, you said you had flushed it," I say.

"You couldn't come to me first? That's not trust. I don't have that trust in you two anymore, especially you, Camille."

I say, "Debbie, I couldn't come to you 'cause you would have denied everything."

She says, "I would not have. I'm your friend. How could you betray me?"

Well, that makes me really angry. That I quote unquote betrayed her seems more important than I did one of the greatest things in my life. I saved her butt.

" "You may hate us, but what we did was an act of true friend- ship." "

I say, "You may hate us, but what we did was an act of true friendship."

"I trusted you," she says.

"Listen, you're gullible. You trust too much. You give in to things."

"You're right," she says. "I trusted you and look what happened!"

I say, "Well, okay. We made a mistake." I'm ready to say anything to get her to stop crying.

"You're right, you made a mistake. And that's the last thing I'm going to say to you!"

And then she leaves. So much for family.

"You're a jerk, Debbie," I call after her. "But just because we dislike you doesn't mean we don't love you."

What do you think?

"They were dead wrong in ratting on Debbie to her parents without confronting her first. They were not good friends."
—student, Springbrook High School, Silver Spring, Maryland

"Camille and Shannon probably don't feel they are important enough to influence Debbie. That could be why they didn't take a shot at talking to her before they went to her parents.

"What happens particularly with young women is they feel insignificant. They can be good friends with each other, but they rely more on men and on adults."
—Jenny Sazama, International Reference Person for Young Adults in Co-Counseling, Teen Empowerment, South End, Boston

"There are differences between the sexes when it comes to interaction with friends. In general females tend to talk more about personal issues. Males talk more about how they're doing in school or sports. There's more bantering and teasing with boys.

"Girls do that less. Girls do more ostracism. If things aren't working, they'll juggle the relationship emotionally by cutting off contact or uniting with somebody who's an enemy."

—Tom Dishion, Ph.D, clinical psychologist, Oregon Social Learning Center, Adolescent Transitions Program, Eugene

steven

moral combat

I'm Seventh Day Adventist. We can't watch TV or anything like that. On Saturdays my best friend, Ralph, and I go bike riding. After a while, Ralph always wants to stop at the mall and play video games like Mortal Kombat or Street Fighter II, Championship Edition.

Ralph isn't a great Christian. He puts a lot of pressure on me and I give in. That night I pray and ask forgiveness. But I know it's partly my fault because I do it every week.

allyson

nothing happened

You know how it always seems that the people you don't like like you, and the people you like never do? At least in my case, that's usually true.

I was surprised when Annie, that's her name, started paying attention to me. Soon we were talking about things that lots of people don't even bring up. Philosophical things and how we dealt with people.

I've always been school-oriented. I've been in gifted programs forever. I'm straitlaced. Annie seemed freer. She was beautiful, too. She told me about places I'll probably never go. One day out of the blue, she said, "Do you believe everyone is bisexual?"

I was seventeen, but nobody had ever asked me that before. I thought, "If I say yes, I'm threatened. If I say no, I've lost everything."

"Well, I guess it's possible."

Annie smiled.

Then I gathered the courage to tell her right to her face how I felt: "Actually I'm in love with you."

"Well, I have feelings for you, too," she said. "Still I need time to make sure, so that nobody gets hurt."

I'm telling you, that was the hardest conversation I'd ever had in my life. I knew I was taking a big risk. I also knew that all my life I'd had crushes. Teachers, baby-sitters, my best friends. Always female. I'd always kind of known about myself.

But I'd never seen any other homosexuals around. I was the only one as far as I could tell. I felt two conflicting pressures: the pressure to conform, to pretend to be straight; the pressure to be who I was.

I argued with myself, "I don't want to step on anyone's toes. Right now, though, I feel optimistic about my life. I'm not a sextrovert; I am homosexual. Is being a lesbian important enough to me to tell people?"

I decided yes. It was time to jump off the cliff.

the note

My best friend, Jessica, knows something is up. We're in chemistry class writing notes to each other.

"What's wrong?" she writes me.

"I think I'm in love," I write back.

"What! I didn't even know you were going out. Anyway, what's wrong with being in love?"

When I don't pass her a note back, she starts guessing why I kept this a secret, especially from her.

"You're in love with a skinhead?"

"No."

"A Birkenstock?"

"No."

"A punk?"

"We're best friends, right?" I finally write.

"A preppy?" Jessica writes back.

"I'm going to be honest with you and I don't want you to freak out."

"An anarchist?"

"NO!" I write in capital letters. "Are you homophobic?"

She doesn't look up. She just writes: "I think people should be who they are."

"I'm in love with a 'she.' "

"I don't care. How's it going? And who is this person?"

"Annie, the one with the wild blond curls."

"Are you going to tell Donna?" Jessica says. I like to share my life with my friends. The three of us have been friends forever. But Donna's nearly a religious fanatic. If I tell her, will she condemn me?

the fallout

After I told Jessica, I opened up to some more people. I tried to keep track of everyone who knew. One of my friends said, "Allyson, this is just a phase you're going through."

I said, "I guess we'll find out."

I did tell Donna and lost her friendship completely. I got a little paranoid. I worried, "Will more friends stop inviting me places? Will conversations change when I show up?"

> " "Will more friends stop inviting me places? Will conversations change when I show up?' "

I walked down the hall at school. A guy I didn't know said, "I hear that chick's a dyke."

His friend looked at me and said, "Homos are sick, man. Get lost. We don't want you here."

I put my head down and kept on walking. I thought, "I'm not evil. I'm not going to corrupt children." I wondered why I got more stress from guys.

From most girls, and some guys, even if they didn't agree with me, I began to receive a certain amount of admiration for being true to myself.

A student named Cathy pulled me aside and said, "I have feelings for a woman. I'm just not sure if I'm willing to act on them."

I told her, "First you should know I believe that having love and showing it is beautiful. But being a lesbian is not just about the physical side of a relationship. It's about feeling more emotionally attached to females than males."

"I've seen you at church," Cathy said. "What do you do about that?"

"That's one of the reasons I had such a hard time coming to terms with myself. I had to choose between believing in this religion, which had been handed to me, and believing in myself.

"I thought, 'My God isn't an angry God. He loves all His children. And there is no kind of love that He doesn't cherish. Sex is just an extra gift He gives us.' "

the risk

I'm one of those people who has to analyze everything so I know what's going on. But my feelings about my sexual orientation couldn't be analyzed.

I needed my mom's advice and help. We've always been close, and I felt bad she didn't know about this major thing in my life. See, this was when I was still thinking I was bisexual. I've come to the conclusion, I'm not.

When my mom said, "Is something wrong?" I said, "I've got to talk to you."

We went into my room; we didn't want to talk in front of my stepdad. She sat down on my floor. And I sat and stared at my carpet for a long time.

Finally I said, "Mom, uh, it's the 's' word, sexuality."

She said, half teasing, "Are you gay?"

"No, I think I'm bisexual."

Then there was one of those silences that seem to last a lifetime.

"Well, those feelings are natural," she said, making it sound like it was okay to be who you were. At that moment I didn't go into details. She didn't ask if there was a person. I didn't tell.

I was just glad to have gotten through that initial hard part. After the conversation, I felt good. I felt I could tell anyone. So I did.

the wrong person

I get home from school and hear the phone ringing. When I answer it, a voice says, "Queers burn in hell."

The next day when I walk out the door to go to school, I can't believe what I see.

The tires on my stepfather's car are slashed. The sidewalk's covered with red letters: DEATH TO ALL DYKES. On the front door the word AIDS is printed in bold letters. The yard is trashed.

My stepdad sees all this and is confused. He's mad, too. I don't think this is the time to tell him I'm a lesbian. Instead I say, "It's a mistake. They must have the wrong person."

I'm scared. I don't go to school that day or the next or the next. I call in sick. I have a room of my own and that's where I stay. It helps me feel normal.

My room has the usual clothes on the floor. Necklaces on my dresser. Stuff at the foot of my coatrack. The Buddhist mandala is still on the wall. So is the poster of the Taj Mahal. I don't know how to handle the situation. I try to rethink what I'm doing. Do I, maybe, have to risk my life for the sake of something that no one can understand? Should I renounce my sexuality, saying it was a phase?

It's easy to give in to pressure. Easier than being alone. But there's nothing wrong with who I am. I should be strong. I must have faith in myself.

That night my mother says, "Why did someone do that to our home?"

"I guess I told the wrong people that I'm a lesbian."

"What's that supposed to mean? You said you had bisexual feelings."

"I'm in love with Annie."

"Annie! What exactly is going on?"

While I'm trying to figure out how to answer her, she says to me, "If you're going to do that"—I'm going to use a profanity here—"if you're going to do that shit, you're not going to live in my house. I'm not going to have any faggots here."

That hurts so much, it's like a slap in the face. I wish she had hit me. I can't believe my own mother has turned on me. But I cannot yell at her. I'd feel guilty. She's been so good to me all my life.

I say, "Nothing happened." That's not true, but I feel that's what she wants to hear.

"Promise me you'll never see her again."

"Okay, I promise." Just saying that tears me up inside. Plus I don't even know how to begin to do that.

I can hear my stepfather yelling my name. "Allyson," he says, "Jessica's on the phone. She wants to talk to you."

Once my mother leaves the room, I tell Jessica everything. "You have to be like that Simon and Garfunkel song, 'I Am a Rock,'" she says. "'A rock feels no pain; an island never cries.'"

I say, "I'm not some tough activist. I'm the person who works underground where the roots are. That makes the job easier for the people further up."

"Does that mean you're in or out of the closet?"

"I refuse to go back in the closet." I say. "The people at school who don't like that will have to learn to live with it. I can't and I won't change."

"What about your mom?"

I say, "I love my mother dearly, but this is one thing where I don't care how she thinks. What matters to me is how you and my good friends think."

"Allyson, I guess that gets us to the last question. Are you going to stop seeing Annie?"

"What do you think?"

What do you think?

"It's harder and more dangerous for a guy to come out of the closet. Allyson shouldn't be worried about what others say. She should be proud of who she is."
  —student, Canarsie High School, Brooklyn, New York

"She should go back in the closet."
  —student, Elkton High School, Elkton, Maryland

"The oppression of gays and lesbians is incredible. But I think, as with other issues in your life, you need to pick and choose your battles. Allyson's not a bad person if she changes her mind and says, 'It was just a

phase.' And it's fine if she wants to stay out of the closet.

"I'd work with her on how hurt she was. How shocked she was that human beings can be like that and trash her home. I'd give her a chance to cry.

"A teen friend could be a good listener for Allyson, too. The friend isn't there to offer advice, but to pay complete and aware attention. The friend is not even interested in the end of the story. What that person wants to do is give Allyson a chance to think through the entire situation."

—Jenny Sazama, International Reference Person for Young Adults in Co-Counseling, Teen Empowerment, South End, Boston

tawanda, mindy, and desiree

getting into trouble with the girls

Tawanda: I'm friends with Mindy and Desiree. We always go into the bathroom at school to smoke and hang out.

Mindy: And talk and talk. At least every Fourth Period.

Desiree: We might not be in the same classes, but we're all together, no matter where we go. We're alike, but different.

Mindy: Like, I live with my brothers, my mother and father. They're the same parents I started out with. My dad owns a business. For all the work he does, it doesn't make much money.

Desiree: That's okay, honey. You're not so different.

Tawanda: My father works nights and my mother's rarely home. He's an alcoholic. My mother was on drugs. Right now she's in a rehabilitation center.

   I have no reason to hide it. All my friends know. Anyway, it's not like I can change my parents. They're old enough to make their own decisions. I live with my father, my brother, my sister, and my niece. I do for myself in my house.

   I like to talk about things that have happened in my life. It helps me get through them.

Desiree: I live with my grandmother. She's good to me. Like, one time I got caught shoplifting. I took a bodysuit. I put it in my book bag. When I walked out, a man grabbed me and made me give him the phone number where I lived.

   That's how my grandmother found out. She said, "Next time if you want something ask me for more money." Then she gave me fifty dollars. I've lived with her for over a year now. Me and my mom and my sister don't get along. It's better this way. It was my mother's idea. She kicked me out. I came home late with Tawanda.

Tawanda: Hello!

Desiree: Okay. So it was six o'clock at night and I was supposed to come right home from school. Instead, I was with my ex-boyfriend. My mother started yelling. She'd never met my boyfriend. I wasn't going to school. I was getting into trouble. "Desiree," she said, "if you don't do what you're supposed to do, you're out of this house." Then she hit me with an extension cord. I've been at my grandmother's ever since.

Mindy: Last year in tenth grade we were ditching a lot. Sometimes we watched TV all day and sometimes we went to school but stayed in the bathroom. We made other friends there, too, all kinds: White. Chinese. Jamaican. Colombian.

Tawanda: You won't hear gossip from me about all that. Desiree, though, she has a big mouth. Don't tell her anything unless you want others to know.

Desiree: Tawanda's intelligent, and she doesn't spread your business.

Tawanda: How I see myself is the advice person. Only Desiree and Mindy don't always listen right away.

Desiree: I was the first one to have sex. I said, "You've got to try it. It's fun, but painful."

Tawanda: And then you pushed me into doing it. You practically threw me in the room and then sat on the bed. I was willing, but that first time ain't no picnic. I bled.

Mindy: The question is, "How do you get the guy to use a condom?"

Tawanda: All together now, you say, "If you want that, first you put on this!"

Desiree: That's what you say now. You didn't say that before I got pregnant.

Tawanda: I gave you advice on the pregnancy. I said, "Start moving. You need help. You should tell your grandmother or mother or somebody."

Desiree: I remember that day. I was going to class.

Tawanda: Right. I'm yelling at you and you're yelling back, "Leave me alone." But I knew where you were going. You went into the bathroom.

Desiree: I was sitting there, crying.

Tawanda: I said, "I'm not going to leave you alone. I'm next to you until you call home."

Desiree: I called my mother and told her. She said, "What are you going to do?" I told her, "I want an abortion." She said, "It's your decision."

Next I called my boyfriend. We both went to the clinic to make sure. He said, "It's your decision." I knew I'd rather hear that than "Keep it."

Tawanda: Or, "So what?" Remember then later I missed a couple periods? I didn't think anything of it. I was, like, it's stress. It'll come tomorrow. Tomorrow.

Desiree: When you told me, I laughed. I said I knew it was going to happen to you. You should have learned from my mistake. But no.

Mindy: Tawanda told me good advice. I was going with this guy. We were always fistfighting. Playing. But sometimes he would get carried away. Tawanda kept telling me to break up with him.

Tawanda: That's right, Mindy. Your attitude completely changed when you were with him. Every time we were in the bathroom, what did you talk about? What you did, how you did it . . .

Desiree: And how many times.

Tawanda: I'd tell you, "Don't go over to his place. Don't call him. Don't speak to him. Forget about him." I must have said it fifty billion times. That's how I give advice. I say it over and over and over until somebody actually listens.

If you see a truck coming down the street, are you going to stand there and let it hit you? You have to move. I'll drill that into your head until you listen.

Mindy didn't listen to me. She got hurt.

Mindy: I got hit so hard when I finally broke up with him. That was his way of showing how much he cared. I guess he thought if he hit me hard enough, I would stay. I knew he was bad news, but I didn't want to see it. Every day I thought he was going to change. And Tawanda kept dragging me into the bathroom, saying, "Leave him."

I get attracted to the wrong people. That's the worst thing about me and my life.

Desiree: I'm not sure what's the best or worst thing for me. I haven't always been paying attention to my life.

Tawanda: My friends and Jamaal, my boyfriend, are the best things for me. We came through a lot of things. Except I won't tell him some of the stuff that I'll tell Mindy and Desiree.

Mindy: Like, you smoke.

Tawanda: Yeah. I still smoke. He didn't want me to drink either, and I stopped. He didn't want me to cut class, and I finally stopped. He's a good influence.

We weren't supposed to be together from the get-go. He's four years older and my father didn't approve of him. He thought Jamaal only wanted me for sex.

Then my father got to know him and now he loves him like a son. His grandmother and mother don't like me, but I could care less. They swear I'm such a bad person; neither of them know me from Eve.

I used to not go to school. Now I do. I'm trying to get myself together. If they don't like me, that's just tough.

Desiree: What we look for in any friend is a lie-free person. All friendships have ups and downs.

Mindy: And times your friends make you crazy.

Tawanda: That's right. But I can't stay mad at friends, especially Desiree and Mindy. It used to be that they could irk a nerve. Lately, though, I grew up. Life was knocking at the door.

Friends are too important to turn into enemies.

Mindy: Actually, Tawanda, when your mother left the house, you calmed down.

Tawanda: Yeah. It's been easier since she went into rehab. A lot of things stopped. I mean, she used to take stuff. Then she'd just disappear for days. After a while I didn't care. I used to wish she would die. She put my family through so much.

Desiree: We all spend far more time with each other than we do with our families.

Mindy: We get out of school at two. I never show up at my house until seven-thirty. Then I go out again at eight-thirty and come back at ten-thirty or so.

My parents never ask me where I am after school. If they do, I say, "I'm going by a friend's house." They used to want the phone numbers. Now I got a beeper.

Desiree: Where do we want to be in ten years? Maybe I'll be a hooker on Forty-second Street, New York, New York. "Here, Daddy, I made seven hundred dollars today." That's a joke.

Tawanda: I can't speak on the future. I got to get out of high school first.

Mindy: I want to do better than my parents do. They make just enough to pay the bills. I see myself in a big mansion with maids, butlers, a nice husband, materialistic stuff, being happy, with a job. I want to have a good career. And a life.

Desiree: Bye.

Mindy: Home.

Tawanda: See you tomorrow.

hector

being different

When I was little, I wanted to be someone else. Someone calm and cool. Instead, the teachers and doctors told my mom and dad I had a learning disorder, A.D.D., attention deficit disorder.

They said, "Hector can't concentrate. Hector can't focus on his work. Give Hector Ritalin to control his hyperactivity."

To me hyperactivity was not really anything. It was running wild. When I started doing something, say, talking, I couldn't stop when people said to stop. And I did everything at a faster pace. I think that's the same for lots of people.

But they gave me Ritalin anyway.

It didn't do jack.

The picking had already started by then. The kids at school acted like I was some jerk-crazy monster. To fit in, everybody had to fit the same image. And I knew no matter how much I might want to be like them, we were different.

We had different opinions. Different feelings. I had a

better sense of right and wrong. I had more compassion. I didn't treat other people like dirt. Kids knew I was an easy target. They figured I'd never fight back.

> # Kids knew I was an easy target.

By the time I was about nine, I was learning to react. One time when I was climbing on the school jungle gym, this kid, this redhead, yelled at me, "Get down. This is white property, you dumb beaner."

I didn't even know for sure what "beaner" meant, but I knew it was something bad. I was ready. "What did you call me?" I said. And then I beat the living crap out of him.

His mom saw us and came charging over. "What are you doing to my son?" she said. I told her exactly what he told me. "My son would never say something like that," she said and walked away with him crying.

After that it seemed like kids would try to get a reaction from me. They thought it was funny to see me fight back.

a shortage of friends

At the age of eleven, sixth grade, I was only three feet four inches tall. The doctors said, when I was born, my pituitary gland got messed up. That gland tells your body how to grow.

"We could put Hector on growth hormones," they said to my parents. I didn't want to be three feet four the rest of my life. I wanted those shots, even though they were terrible.

At first my mom gave them to me. Eventually, I had to give them to myself. Every day. Once the needle exploded in my arm. After a while, the kids found out about the shots. Some were jealous. They wished they were taller.

Others, like this guy Dirk, saw it as a new opportunity to pick at me. He was standing by the doorway to our classroom. He kept saying, "You're a spoiled baby. Your parents give you everything."

I said, "Dirk, leave me alone."

"Growth hormones? You're on steroids," he said.

"I'd shut up if I were you."

"Hey, Hector, you getting those big cysts on your arms from the steroids?" And with that he pulled off my glasses and threw them across the room. I walked over and picked them up. They were bent in half, nearly broken.

By then I knew I couldn't give up on a fight until the person was down or I was unconscious. "Don't mess with me," I said, and I pushed him hard. I flew at him, wrapped my arm around his neck, and started pounding him in the face.

He grabbed me around my midsection and shoved me against the wall. I smashed his head into the doorframe. And then he got me against the wall again.

My head caught on a nail that was sticking out. It left

a big gash. There were a whole bunch of people watching this, cheering. They loved the blood. A teacher came up and said, "Hector, what did you do?"

"Do what? I didn't do anything," I said. Dirk just smiled. After I got five stitches, they told me I was suspended.

easing the pain

One day Andy, a new kid in my ninth-grade chemistry class, sees me punching the concrete wall behind the school. He says, "Why are you doing that?"

"Why not?" I say. "It's fun. I've had a couple hairline fractures."

"What about playing bloody knuckles?"

"That's not for me," I say. "I'm a no muss, no fuss kind of guy. Anybody gets in my face, I beat 'em down."

"But you always get hurt."

"Not always, just mostly," I tell him.

By then I love to fight. The growth hormones are working, too. I'm larger, nearly five feet tall. I have a better range. I'm able to fight more aggressively. It feels good beating up people.

They have done me a disservice. I'm giving it back.

I find it relieving.

They have inflicted emotional pain on me.

I'm just turning it around, giving them physical pain. In a typical month I'm in twenty fights.

reprogramming

The doctors say to my mom and dad, "Hector seems to lack the necessary skills he needs for making friends. Let's put him on a special kind of lithium to control his spontaneous reactions."

That means I'm on Ritalin for the hyperactivity, the growth hormone shots, and now lithium. I start having these tremors. I can't even hold my pencil.

"I'm not taking that stuff anymore," I tell them. "And I'm done with those stupid shots, too. I'm sixteen years old. I'm five feet four. I'll live with that."

The doctors say, "Well, maybe the shots did have some side effects. Maybe they made you a little angry."

My parents say, "Hector, would you like to see an acupuncturist?"

The first thing the acupuncturist does is agree I should be taken off all my medicines and put on these herbal things. I tell her, "I don't like most kids my age. My main friend, Andy, is not really a friend. He's more somebody that I don't dislike.

"The two of us stay away from the rest of the people at school. Neither of us gets along with many of them. Andy and I spend a lot of time playing a game called Shadow Run. He's more nutso-freaky than I am when it comes to fighting."

The acupuncturist says, "Fighting gets you nowhere."

She makes arrangements for me to work with abused and abandoned dogs and cats in an animal shelter. I take this sheepdog the size of a washing machine out for a walk. He starts running down the hill with me behind him. When I catch up, I ask him why he ran. He makes me laugh.

I love animals more than people. Animals are more caring. They love to be loved, and then they love back. I tell the acupuncturist I'd like to go to medical school. "Why not veterinary school?" she says.

"I don't like to see animals get cut open, even if it's helping them. And I could never put a dog or cat to sleep. I don't feel that way about most people."

"Try to ignore what people say. Just don't listen," she says. "Think about something else. Something that makes you happy. Program yourself."

The next time a kid pushes my buttons, I try to walk away. When it's really bad, I go to the Y and work out. I pretend the weights are the person I'm mad at. I just pump and pump and pump until I can't go anymore.

If I can't do that, I pick up a book that'll put me in a different world. I read science fiction and fantasy books.

I tell myself about the good things in my life. I'm bright. I have good parents. I have a great sister. I have a future if I can keep my act together.

Some days it works. Some days it doesn't. But I'm glad I am who I am. I've been dealt a bad hand, still I'm making it all right.

I'm Hector, the one and only. The flash.

What do you think?

"Kids are cruel. It's no secret that people who are different are going to get mocked out. I hate to admit it, but I'd go along with the group and not stand up for Hector."

—student, Smith School, Ramsey, New Jersey

"People who make fun of you are doing it to escape their own problems. Turn the tables. Start asking them about themselves and don't talk so much about yourself. Don't be bossy, snotty, or put them down."

—student, Crater High School, Central Point, Oregon

"I've never met a person who doesn't have some positive aspect. Hector should find that about himself, then look for others who share his interest.

"He was dealt a bad hand in a way that wasn't his fault. It's part of the world, and the world of friendship is not always fair. Some of what happens to him with peers is just not in his control.

"The good news is that adolescence is probably the worst time for him. When he gets to be an adult, maybe goes to college, there are all sorts of people to connect with."

—Tom Dishion, Ph.D., clinical psychologist, Oregon Social Learning Center, Adolescent Transitions Program, Eugene

cheating

"You're going to be my maid of honor," Mia said to me. We were best friends. For a week straight in sixth grade we went and looked at all these wedding things. We picked out our perfect marriage gowns and bridesmaid stuff.

"You're going to be my maid of honor, too," I said.

We were always together. We went to the mall, to the beach, to the movies. We picked up boys. Mia was always there for me. She knew in my mind I had this ideal, the perfect husband. "He'll be tall, blond, and most likely named Alan," I told her. "And he'll be able to pick me up."

Looking back, now, it's weird, since the boyfriend who caused the whole incident was just like that. His name was Alan. He was about two hundred some pounds, six foot three, with short, blond hair. He could even pick me up. "Perfect," I thought.

mr. imperfect

I met up with Alan in ninth grade. He was friends with a guy Mia was dating. When we first started going out, Alan was dating someone else, too. That got over and pretty soon he was seeing me solely.

It felt good to be protected. You know, "I have a boyfriend. Just leave me alone." He gave me the affection I wanted. I liked to be hugged and told, "I love you." It made me feel good about myself.

Mia had no problem with that until Alan started taking me away from her. She said, "You're always with Alan. We have no friendship left."

> " "You're always with Alan. We have no friendship left.""

I knew she was right. I was obsessed with him. In his own way, he was obsessed with me, too. He limited my friends. He started having me clock in. I had to tell him where I was going, even when it was the grocery store. He wanted to know all the details and then he didn't believe me.

He was constantly telling me, "You're a slut." I'd try to hold a civil conversation with him and it would end up in a yelling match. Then we'd have sex.

I'd call up Mia crying, "Our relationship is just about sex. We can't talk."

"Why do you stay with him?"

"It's, like, I have this ideal that's set in my mind. 'He's Alan, he's tall, he can pick me up,'" I said. Then I started crying.

"Get away from him," she said.

I listened to her. I broke up with him. I broke up with him so many times until he'd say, "Bethany, I've changed. I've changed." Then I'd go back with him.

Mia said, "You're never there for me."

"I'm there when I can be. I'm sorry."

impure thoughts

Alan starts the pushing stuff about six months after we begin dating. It isn't real hitting, hitting. At least not except for a couple times when he hits me. Other than that it's basic grabbing and yelling.

I tell Mia about it, but what's she going to do? She wants me to get away from him. She just doesn't know how to get me to do it.

Then one day, she says, "Alan would cheat on you. Believe me."

"No, he wouldn't. He'd never do something like that. He always says to me, 'I'll never cheat on you.'"

She says, "Bethany, am I your best friend?"

"Sure," I say.

"A best friend knows you the most. At times a best friend even knows you more than you know yourself."

She has my attention.

"If a best friend is telling you something, it is obviously something that needs to be heard."

I start crying. I cried probably a poolful. "What am I doing?" I say. "I don't think I've had a pure thought since I started going with Alan."

"What's that supposed to mean?" Mia says.

"Like, I really envy my sister. She goes to that Christian college. She has a perfect relationship with her boyfriend. No sex. They're on a good track. I want something like that."

"So break up with Alan."

"You're right," I say. "He has no type of guidance. What I'm doing with him is wrong. I want to get back to Christian values."

"But, Bethany, you know you don't like church. You say it bores you."

"What I mean is before I go home from being with Alan, I have to put mints in my mouth because I've been drinking. Something's wrong if I constantly have to hide what we do."

Mia says, "That's what I've been trying to tell you for a year. Why don't we go to the beach for the weekend? The way we used to, when we were both single."

We go to the beach, meet two guys, and I cheat on Alan.

"Good," Mia says. "I'm glad you did it. I want you to get away from him."

"I know," I say. "But I feel guilty."

"Forget it," she says. "It isn't someone Alan knows."

"I've never lied to him."

"Today's a good time to start."

the payback

Mia and I had just gotten home from the beach. She was still at my house when I called Alan. He was over in five minutes and he lives a half hour away.

Alan and I went out for a drive. After we parked, I said, "Listen, I don't want to date you anymore."

"Why?" he said.

"I don't want the hassle of having a boyfriend. Also, I did cheat on you. I'm sorry."

He flipped out. He didn't hit me at first. There was a lot of screaming instead. Then he grabbed me. He was very physical. Suddenly, though, he quieted down and said, "It doesn't matter you cheated on me, because Mia is good, too."

"I don't believe you," I said. I thought to myself, "He's saying that to hurt me."

He said, "You know that time you had to baby-sit your little sister? I stopped by Mia's. Maybe we didn't have sex, but we sure did other things."

I couldn't believe what I was hearing.

My heart cracked in half.

Everything ached.

I started to cry.

But still, I cheated on him. I took it as my payback. Then I started thinking, "Mia is my best friend. She's been my best friend for five years now. She knows how much I love Alan. How can she do that, then turn around and say she wants me to get away from him?" I tried to remember exactly when she said he'd cheat on me.

When Alan dropped me off back to my house, I walked through the door and Mia was still there. I looked upset, but she expected that. She was worried that when I told him I wanted to break up, he'd hit me.

She had no idea he'd tell me about the two of them. I wasn't going to say anything that minute. It was an inappropriate time. I was hurt. But my mom was there. One of her friends was there. I'd wait.

For some reason, I kept dating Alan after all.

the heartbreak

A month later Mia and I are painting our toenails, talking. I'm realizing, "This is my best friend. She wouldn't fool around with Alan to hurt me."

I'm not going to be nasty. I make mistakes. Everyone does. The whole conversation sort of pops out. "So, Mia, I hear that you and Alan hooked up."

Silence.

"Mia, you heard me," I say.

"I don't know what you're talking about," she says.

"Please, don't play the dumb bit. I know about it," I say.

She's, like, "He told you? I can't believe that he told you."

I'm thinking, "I can't believe that you even did that for him to tell me. Where's your excuse? Where's your I'm sorry?" I guess she's not saying she's sorry since I'm not crying. I'm not steaming up, getting ready to throw something at her.

I won't do that, anyway. I don't think very much of her at this point, but she is my best friend.

Still, she's just shrugging it off, like I don't care. I do. Finally I say to her, "Exactly what happened?"

"It was no big deal," she says.

"Tell me how it happened."

She says, "Are you sure?"

"Yes."

"Well, he came over to my house and said, 'Let's go out.' We went for a drive. He kept asking me to do stuff. Finally I said, 'Okay.' "

I'm thinking, "You could have said no!"

Alan and I keep dating for another few months after that conversation with Mia. She says, "Bethany, Alan's controlling you."

Why should I listen after what she's done?

One year, two months, three weeks, and one day after our first date, it's finished. It's hard for me to get away from Alan. The last time we break up, he threatens to kill me.

the failed reunion

After the relationship with Alan really did end, I went to Mia. I wanted someone to fill the place that was now empty. I called her up and said, "Alan and I are over forever!"

"That's great," she said.

"I need you back in my life," I said. "And I'm going to be there for you all the time. We're going to get our friendship back on track."

There was this funny silence.

"What's the deal?" I said.

Silence.

"Are you seeing somebody?" I said.

"Well, yes," she said.

"So tell me. Who is it?"

"His name is Josh."

"You mean the Josh we knew in middle school?" I said.

"Yeah."

"The guy was always rude and ignorant to me, and to everyone else."

"He was probably joking around," she said.

"Mia, I'm your friend. I know this guy. Please do not hook up with him. If you're going to talk to him, talk to him. But do not do anything else."

The next thing I knew she was obsessed with him and I was left in the dust, not able to pick up with my best friend.

the future

In my school people worry most about what they're going to do this weekend or who they're going to get drunk with. I'm always, like, whatever the crowd is doing. Now I want to change.

I pray I meet someone with Christian values. Bingo. I notice a guy named Matt and start flirting with him. Unfortunately the other guys in my school take it upon themselves to tell him about me and Alan. Plus he wasn't quite the only one.

Matt doesn't believe it at first. He's never had sex and doesn't plan on having sex in any other relationship besides marriage. I feel bad. I want to say, "No, I haven't ever had sex." I want to be a virgin for him. Instead, I have to say, "I want to be, but I'm not."

He says, "I'm disappointed, but everyone makes mistakes. I don't think less of you."

I want to tell Mia about my discussion with Matt. I want her to be part of my life. I want her to know I'm finally doing everything right.

I want to tell her that I think a girlfriend and a boyfriend are no different. The boyfriend has to be your friend, too. You have to be able to talk. And it should feel as good to talk to him as it does to talk to a girlfriend. Although you're showing your boyfriend affection that you're not showing your girlfriend, I think the value of the friendship shouldn't be much different.

I call her up, but I don't get to tell her any of this. She interrupts before I begin. She's planning her wedding. To Josh. What we talked about as kids is gone. She doesn't say a word about me being her maid of honor.

megan

sweet revenge

If my outside were like my inside, I'd be this scrawny person with owlish glasses. But in reality I have a lot of red hair and a size double D chest. I developed quickly, between tenth and eleventh grade.

Suddenly guys started watching me. It was overwhelming. At first I assumed they were making fun of me. But then it was happening all the time.

I realized that in high school many guys are much more interested in a girl's looks and her figure than her personality. I mean, you could have a horrible personality, but if you look like Dolly Parton, those guys' brains turn off.

They're like dogs seeing a bone. They start barking.

Every single day as I go from calculus to physics to English, I pass these groups of guys who make sounds through their teeth and say original things like, "Damn, look at her tits."

"What's your number, baby?"

"My friend here likes you."

I try to ignore them, but sometimes they put their hands on me. They do it in a crowd so I don't really know who does it. Other times they follow me. They block my way. Once this obnoxious guy stood in my path with his arms extended. He was laughing with his friends.

I said, "Excuse me," pushed by him, and kept on going. I don't want to say anything back just because I don't want to.

Having this kind of thing happen has made me wary of boys in general. A couple guys I know as good friends, like one named Grant and another named Ben. But I've never had a serious boyfriend. I don't even date very much. I worry about date rape.

Instead, I study a lot. I don't drink. I never have and never will smoke or do drugs. I'm a quiet person. Still I like looking in the mirror and liking what I see. It makes me feel good about myself.

I don't wish I were ugly.

I just wish I could be pretty without this other stuff.

black angora sweater

I have—or had—two best girlfriends, Jennifer and Robyn. We've known each other since middle school computer science class. Jennifer has my same problem and experiences. We help each other.

But with Robyn, all of a sudden she starts saying I shouldn't wear my black angora sweater that's gorgeous and I love. Plus my grandparents bought it for me. She says, "You know, Megan, it's too small for you."

I say, "Well, no, actually it isn't. It's my size. I just happen to have a big chest. That's how I look in sweaters and there's nothing I can do about it."

"Then you shouldn't wear it," she says.

"What do you want me to do, Robyn? Wear my dad's size?"

"Yeah."

That makes me even madder. She's trying to place the blame on me for the guys' actions. In fact, I've already made lots of changes in my life to see if that makes a difference.

I have some other sweaters I don't wear to school, ever. I don't wear any tight jeans at all. I never wear anything low cut. In the winter I have this huge peacoat that was my father's. I put that on. If it's hot weather, I carry my books in front of my chest.

Some days I take detours, go different routes. I don't look at the guys I have to pass. If I see Grant or Ben around, I say, "Wait for me," and I walk with them. I find that if I'm with someone who's big and male, I'm usually left alone.

I think it's pathetic that I do all this.

"Give me a break," Robyn says. "You wouldn't dress provocatively if you didn't like the attention."

I'm so insulted. How could another girl, let alone a best friend, say that?

feeling like garbage

Jennifer says, "Being hassled is so widespread, it's sort of an expected thing. This is what happens. You just put up with it."

"Have you ever considered telling anybody?" I ask her.

"Megan," she says, "that's ludicrous. What can they do? Make this an all-girls school?"

"I guess you're right. There'd be a lot of negative reactions even from people we know. Say, we went in and talked to some authority figure. Put our names to this problem. I bet some of them would think, 'Oh, you're totally antimale, militant feminists.'"

"You wouldn't dress provocatively if you didn't like the attention."

A few days after Jennifer and I had this conversation, she comes to me and is literally shaking. She's wearing this pretty burgundy dress with a cowl neck. She tells me she was walking outside the school, when these two guys started following her, saying to each other, "How much would you pay for her?"

She felt in real danger. She began walking faster, looking for anyone she knew heading for school. When she found Grant, she walked with him. The other two guys lost interest.

"That does it," I tell her. "I'll go with you to the counselor."

"I just don't think it would make any difference," Jennifer says.

"What if we get them to do a presentation, like the kind we had on how drugs kill you?" I say.

Jennifer says, "Forget it, Megan. We already had one on respecting each other, and I think that's a big part of the problem. A lot of guys want to show off for each other. If they cared for women in general, they wouldn't be doing this. For some reason they want to make us feel like garbage."

"There's a law here against sexual harassment. It applies to high school students, too."

"I know that," she says. "But they'd have to arrest half the school. I don't want to be a test case. I don't want publicity. I just want it to go away."

sleeping dogs

Jennifer came up to me after school. "Robyn's been on the phone, crying to me, Grant, and some of our other friends. She says she's embarrassed to go to the mall with you 'cause all these guys stare at you. It's humiliating.

"She says you're getting to be such a slut. Your personality has completely changed. Isn't it terrible, blahblahblah."

I was in shock. I thought of calling those same friends and saying, "If Robyn says anything again, please tell me." Then Robyn called me. I put aside my anger and decided, "Let sleeping dogs lie." I didn't bring it up. But I know I sounded cold.

I started spending less time with her. She wasn't a fun friend to me. Next, Grant weighed in with his two cents and said, "Megan, no matter what, best friends should always stay together. You've deserted Robyn."

I was upset. I wanted to scream, "Deserted Robyn after what she did to me?" Instead, I went to my friends for a reality check. "Do I look cheap?" I asked them.

They all said, "No, that's not how you come across. You look sexy in sweaters, but there's nothing you can do about it. It's your body type."

hu-mongous revenge

"Jennifer," I say, "you know what I want? Revenge!" Then we both start laughing.

"Right! Let's get a giant boxing glove, walk up, punch them out, and vanish."

"Wait," I tell her. "I have a better idea. We'll get this

hu-mongous water gun filled with paint. Walk into school and whoever says anything lousy to us, *blam*. Head to toe, bright pink."

"Sweet revenge."

I'm still smiling as I head toward my car at the end of the day. In the distance, I notice Robyn. She's bleached her hair very blond. I can't believe it!

I keep on walking until I pass this guy. He says, "You know what? You really have some tits."

I stop. This guy is not someone you'd ever want to have a conversation with. He's not someone you'd ever want to go out with. You immediately wonder, "Why did he even evolve if this is all he can do with himself?"

Does he think I'm going to say, "What a charming thing to say. Please, please, take me out."

Since I never say anything, I sometimes think, "Do these guys just assume I never will?"

Today is different. I say to him, "My gosh, your penis looks larger. Did you stuff your pants with a sock? Jerk." He definitely looks surprised.

I know that doesn't help solve this issue, but as I walk away it sure makes me feel better.

What do you think?

"Boys like that are just ignorant. But her so-called friend Robyn wasn't any better."
  —student, Laurel High School, Laurel, Maryland

"Megan should report it. Get the guys in trouble for the trouble they cause her."
  —student, Cleveland High School, Portland, Oregon

our tattoos

I guess this guy Alex is the one person I confide in. Over a period of time we've had a lot of the same problems. School. Stepdads who are recovering alcoholics. Busboy jobs at Jolly Jack's. Drug rehab.

We're both from Catholic families, too, but neither of us believes in religion. I think religion is manmade. I do believe in a god, though. And hopefully, there's a spiritual afterlife. I'd like to believe that spirits are free and roam the earth.

The first time me and Alex really got our moms upset was when we came home drunk with our first tattoos. His was a skull with a top hat and a cane behind it. Mine was this smiling face with two horns growing out of the forehead. Underneath was written LITTLE DEVIL.

We both get tired of adults jumping on us about how we look. We'll throw on a pair of holey jeans, with raggedy old shirts. They're comfortable. We think people should be allowed to be who they want to be. Without any criticism.

With Alex it's more than friends, it's like brothers.

With the other guys, there are about four to ten of us, we just hang together. It depends on who's home and who has to do what. I call around, get everybody together, and figure out something to do.

Maybe we go up to the mall. Maybe we go to the pool hall. Maybe we just go down the street and wait for the rivalries to come around. You could say we're in our juicing phase. And lately I feel like it's a hostile environment.

The cops are everywhere, waiting for us to pop up with an assault-and-battery here and there. Waiting for someone to call in with a report. They're around the corner ready to catch us.

The cops are acting like we're as serious as the Bloods or the Crips. Every once in a while somebody gets shot. But that's it. I mean, most of us are in school.

life mismanagement

A couple weeks ago I was in my Life Management class. I'd taken it four times, so I didn't think it mattered I hadn't gone for the last five days.

When I came in, the teacher was on my case. He got an attitude and pushed me down into a chair. I didn't like that too much. We almost got in a fight.

Instead, I decided to leave school for the rest of the day. And there was Alex. His mom was dropping him off. I went up and said, "Let's get out of here. Go to John's."

He lived right down the road. He had a suspended license from a drug deal.

When we got there, John said, "Harry, wanna go driving around for a while? You can drive my car."

It was a great day, oh yeah. The sun was out. I was having fun driving. It was a Jeep Cherokee. We got hooked up with some marijuana, twenty-three grams, almost an ounce. We were going to sell it!

"The cops!" I said. I could see the flashing light in the rearview mirror. They were signaling us to pull over.

"You boys skipping school?" the one cop said. Just then I guess they saw Alex shoving something under the seat.

"Mind if we search your car?" the other cop said.

"Go ahead," John said. They found the marijuana.

"You boys skipping school?" the one cop said.

Then it was "Show me your license" and "Spread-eagle against the side of the car." They cuffed us. Read us our rights. They put us in the back of their car and kept us there for about three hours. None of us said anything the whole time.

I was angry for the fact that I had gotten caught. And I

knew how pissed my mom was going to be. Finally they took us downtown to the county jail. They booked us and said, "We're charging you with possession and intent to sell."

doing time thinking

John's mom bailed him out right away. Me and Alex were put on the same floor. He was in East Wing and I was in West Wing. It was rough.

Most of the prisoners were grown men. There were a lot of fights. Then they'd talk, play cards, and go back to sticking to themselves.

I started thinking about another time me and Alex had been caught doing something. Three years ago. We were fourteen. We'd been partying and everything. We wanted to go joyriding.

We stole a Cavalier and it ran out of gas. We took a Honda Accord. The person who owned it woke up and reported it stolen. We were, like, a block away when the police stopped us. They didn't take us to jail. They just scared us. Our parents had to come pick us up from the police station at three in the morning. At the time we were going to a Catholic school, so everybody was, like, Wow.

That was then. Now I was counting the sixth day, the seventh day in jail, wondering when my parents would decide to bail me out. Alex had freaked. His parents bailed him out.

I had nothing to do but more thinking. I realized I didn't really look up to none of my friends. Not even Alex. I didn't see any of them going anywhere quick.

We were, like, the bad crowd, I guess.

Just before I'd been caught that first time, for the stolen car, I'd had a girlfriend, Andrea. She was the only person I ever showed my poetry. I write a lot of poetry. Depending on my mood, I write poems about anger or fear or love. Pure reality. In a way, she was the only person I looked up to. She stood by what she believed in. I liked that in a person.

We had to split up because of her mother. They were fancy people and her mother didn't approve of me. "Harry's a hoodlum," she said to Andrea. She treated me like I was this completely bad kid that was going to ruin her daughter's life.

That upset me. I think of myself as sometimes being in the wrong place at the wrong time doing something that I shouldn't have been doing. I don't really go out looking for trouble. It just follows me.

getting out and getting on

On the ninth day my mom bails me out. I come home to be yelled at. "I can't believe you went out and were messing with drugs," my mom says. "I can't believe that you were even around it."

I call Alex. "What's happening?" I say.

"Harry, my parents are saying you're a bad influence. You're evil."

"What!"

"I'm not supposed to even talk to you."

"Okay, okay," I say, "but I think everybody's got their own mind to choose what they want to do. If I influence them, that's their choice to be influenced. I don't pressure anybody."

"I know that," Alex says. "But still the public defender suggested not to have any contact with you until after court."

I say, "You sound like him. He told me the same thing. It's just that, you know, I don't trust too many people. You're, like, the one person I really trust. And now I'm not allowed to have contact with you. It sucks."

"Yeah," he says, "it sucks. But the cops have been driving by my house."

"My mom thinks a bunch of drug dealers are going to come to my house. She had the number changed." I tell him the new number and hang up, frustrated.

There are only two people allowed to come over, according to my mother. One's this guy, Damien. I haven't hung out with him in a long time. He's a Goody Two-Shoes. The other's my girlfriend, Heather.

I've been going out with her off and on for about two and a half years. She lives down the street. I see her, I guess, three times a week. What does she think about my getting busted? I don't know. We haven't talked about it. She hasn't asked, and I've learned not to tell her things. They always seem to come creeping and crawling back from other people that I don't want to know. Like, her mom and mine are friends.

I sort of miss Alex. The one person I trust and I'm not supposed to see him. I won't. I don't want to cause any problems in his house.

I'm working two jobs right now. I just got hired to be a busboy at Chuck E. Cheese, too. There's a chance me and Alex'll get jail time. It's up to the judge. I heard from my public defender that hopefully we'll be getting a bunch of probation and a lot of fines.

If that happens, maybe I'll call up old Alex and say, "Do you think everything would have been different if we hadn't gotten those first tattoos?"

ashley

the contract

I'm sitting in the student lounge with my friends, when Cynthia, a girl I know, goes running by screaming, "Where's that *#$%!* Janice? I'm gonna kill her!" You can tell she's ready to hit the roof. She's not pretending.

Our school isn't the worst, but some disturbance happens every day. Most times it's, "He say, she say. She looked at me the wrong way. He gritted on me first."

About two years ago a guy got beaten so bad he had to be helicoptered out. After that the school decided to try peer mediation to stop fights before they get dangerous. Now I'm a trained mediator, but when Cynthia runs by, I'm thinking more about my own problems.

Leslie's been my best friend nearly five years, since eighth grade. We're both on the lacrosse team. I'm also a majorette. I'm really close to two of the other majorettes, too. If all four of us are, say, at lunch together, lately Leslie feels left out. I guess she's jealous. She thinks they're taking me away from her.

This particular day Tommy, my boyfriend, is on one

side of me, and I hear Leslie saying to him, "I hate when they ignore me and act like life's only about being a majorette."

Tommy says, "Don't worry. They ignore me all the time," which isn't true. In these conversations he never knows what's going on 'cause he's a guy.

Usually he's understanding. We're solid. The main time we're alone together is Friday nights. Besides that, we both work, have school, sports, and the other usual stresses.

I'm getting ready to tell him and Leslie that they can't be mad every time I talk about majorettes, when Mrs. Gifford the mediator trainer comes up. She says, "Ashley, we need you at the mediation center."

the mediation

When I walked into the center, there was Cynthia and Janice. I knew both of them, but I knew Cynthia better. She was so angry, she could barely sit still.

Right away I started telling them the mediation rules. "You know my name's Ashley. I'm your mediator. You have a dispute, so you're called the disputants.

"The biggest rule is that you two agree that even if it's the end of the day, the bell rings, and you've been in here since eight-thirty, you can't go home until you solve your problem.

"During the mediation process, you can't talk to each

other. Only speak directly to me. This is not a rush thing. You'll each get your own amount of time. You have to pay attention to what's going on in the actual process. I'll be taking notes the whole time. And, also, you're not allowed to cuss.

"Who'd like to go first?"

Sometimes no one does. I've sat there in silence for ten minutes. I can't say, "Well, you go first," because then they could say, "Ashley showed favoritism."

This time, though, Cynthia was fired up enough to start. "I'm here because I know if I don't try to do something through mediation, I'll beat Janice bloody and end up suspended. And it shouldn't be my fault."

Basically what happened was this: Cynthia and Janice are best friends. Cynthia has a boyfriend named Nate. They're all at a party together, but Janice has to get home. It's past her curfew. Nate offers to take her. On the way, he stops at his house and they have sex.

Nate comes back to the party and acts normal. Then that morning, right before school, someone tells someone who tells Cynthia what happened. Cynthia is furious. How could her best friend do that?

"Is Nate a student here?" I asked Cynthia.

"No," she said.

If he had been, we would have called him into the mediation center, too. He was the prime mover of the whole situation. Next, I said to Janice, "Do you understand what Cynthia's saying?"

"Yes."

"Can you repeat it?"

Piece by piece Janice had to tell me what Cynthia had just said. "Now, Janice, how do you explain this?" Janice knew what she did. She knew she couldn't lie her way out of it. The only thing she could say was, "I did it."

It was intense.

Cynthia stood up and looked like she was about to kick Janice's butt. Janice was so scared, she jumped up and moved clear around the table. Janice is the kind who gets into arguments, says, "Yeah, I'll be there at that time," then never shows up.

Cynthia's feisty. She'd just as soon shoot Janice's head off if she ever went near Nate. More than once that day Mrs. Gifford had to come in and take Cynthia out of the room to calm her down.

In my heart I knew if I were in that situation, if Tommy slept with Leslie, I'd be furious. But the mediator can never take sides. I wasn't allowed to suggest a solution, either. I couldn't say, "Maybe you can agree to do it this way."

What I had to try to do was get Cynthia and Janice to understand what they'd done wrong, why they had this conflict, and how they could solve it. If they solved the dispute themselves, they could learn from it. Then, maybe, the problem wouldn't happen again.

After four hours in the mediation room, they came to an agreement. At school Cynthia and Janice would have no contact. Janice would not interfere with Cynthia and Nate anymore. Janice had to stay away, in her own world. Cynthia could do anything she wanted about Nate.

I'm still trying to get over the hurt for what Janice did.

Whatever they all did outside of school was their own business. We couldn't stop or monitor that. I wrote that on these long sheets of blue paper. They were the official contract made in four copies.

I told them, "You both have to sign these. Under each of your names I'm going to write. 'This is what we have agreed to.' If you fail to do what's on this sheet, like, if you're caught talking on school grounds after you've agreed you can't have any contact, you can be suspended or even expelled from school.

"A copy of this contract will go to the counselor, to the principal, and one each to you."

the reality

It's a week later. Cynthia comes into the mediation center. She says, "I'm still trying to get over the hurt from what Janice did. There's anger in me and I bet in Janice, too."

They haven't spent any time with each other since

that day. And I feel they're going to stay clear on their own pathways. "What about you and Nate?" I say.

"I've talked to him. He thinks I've forgotten the whole thing. He keeps saying, 'Why won't you kiss me?' I say, 'Why would I want to?'

"I'm going to keep him hanging on a string. Play hard to get. He deserves for me to be mean to him. He says, 'Cynthia, baby, I want you back.' I say, 'No way.' "

I know that's a normal teenage response for a girl. But I don't see myself doing that. I think learning how to use mediation has made the difference. It's taught me to go to a friend when I have a problem with them.

Before mediation I didn't really talk out my differences with friends. I kind of let them be. I lost friends that way. Now I speak up about our difficulties. In fact, I'm on my way to sit down with Leslie to straighten out her bad feelings about me and the majorettes.

lola

a family of friends

I'm Chinese. My family came to the United States when I was three. For the next ten years we lived in a crime-ridden neighborhood where people were likely to die suddenly and violently.

In kindergarten I was walking home from school wearing a T-shirt with a happy face on it. A junkie stopped me and asked, "Do you have any dope?" I didn't know the happy face was that week's code to identify drug dealers.

Today the memory shocks me, that somebody thought anyone as young as I was, was selling drugs. But at the time I didn't think much of it.

the bond

Some of my friends' parents are drug addicts. Some are alcoholics. Some are never home. My dad is in and out of my life as he pleases. My mom at least is home, but she is

146

emotionally unstable. She becomes violent toward me and sometimes my sisters.

She beats us if we argue back, if we don't bring home all A's, don't cook, don't clean, don't pay bills on time. For a long time I think it's my fault I get beaten so much.

My friends and I don't talk much about our family life with one another.

When I am in third grade, my best friend, Jacquetta, dies. Jacquetta and I had done all those little-kid things together. We'd swung on the swings. We'd skipped rocks in the river. We'd played tag, ball, hide-and-go-seek. I ask everybody, "What happened to Jacquetta?" Nobody will talk to me about it.

A friend finally says, "There's a suspicion Jacquetta's dad beat her to death."

I feel isolated. If you lose your best friend and you don't really have family support, who do you have?

The kids in my neighborhood become my extended family. We know the pain and anger we feel living in a violent environment. We all stick together. There is a bond. With each other we seek and find the love and the friendship we need.

One day a bunch of us are on the bus going downtown. This bee starts buzzing around the seats, and we all try to smash it. My neighbor, Amber, who at seven years old is really religious, stands up and says, "Let it be. All God's creatures deserve to live."

We're so touched by her eloquent speech, we don't kill the bee. Instead we open the window to let it fly out. I'll always remember how her words moved me.

the conflict

My elementary school was predominantly African-American. Of seven hundred students, there were ten Asian kids from three different families.

Little kids don't look at a person's skin color. All I knew was I kind of liked the fact I stood out from the crowd. I was considered smart by my friends. Once in a while they teased me. Like, an African-American boy named Derek would call me "Miss Goody Two-Shoes."

We had a class together. He was smart but never studied. He didn't have much self-esteem. I had a lot of faith in both of us. I looked up to him, and I guess that's one of the things that encouraged our friendship. In some ways Derek looked up to me, too.

He became my "big brother." We didn't really consider it a gang in elementary school. It was kind of like a clique, and Derek was the leader. He'd say, "Kids respect you, Lola. They'd like to achieve in school as much as you do."

I did well in athletics, too. My father had wanted a boy. By the time they got to me, the fourth child, he and my mom figured I was going to be the last. From a young age, I was treated as a son. I was allowed to climb trees, take karate, and go on father-son outings.

When my friends picked teams, I was the first girl chosen, even ahead of some boys. Derek encouraged me. He taught me how to throw like a guy.

Some of the Asian boys got beaten up, but I only got

into fights a few times. After school if Derek, Amber, and the other kids couldn't find me, they'd knock on my door. They'd say to my mother, "Is Lola here? Can she come out?"

My parents had unspoken but obvious racism. They didn't like me spending my free time with African-American kids. They worried that I would be forced to join a gang.

They said to my friends, "Lola has no time to play."

"They are my friends," I said to my parents. "I want to be with them."

In my mind, I was making a whole speech: "These are the kids I'm growing up with. We see each other every day at school, and here in the projects. This neighborhood is only so big. We want to be together in our world.

"Being with friends is a happier place. It's more fun than at home. We feel safer. Our friends will stand up for us. We will fight for each other.

"Sometimes we get in a fight with each other. But when something dangerous is about to happen, we know we'll be there for one another. That's more than we can say for our families. And people wonder why kids join gangs."

In reality, I said nothing.

After I got beaten again, my parents would say, "Practice your calligraphy. You need to perfect your brush stroke."

lost kids

Just after I am named Outstanding Student in seventh grade, my parents announce two things. We kids are moving with our mother into an apartment on the other side of town. My parents are officially separating.

"And we forbid you to come back to see your friends in the projects," they tell me. "They are bad influences."

"They are my family, more than you are," I say. I don't care if my parents beat me. I am crying so much anyway. Because of them, I must move away from the only friends I've really ever known and into a new school.

This new one has many Asian students. It's more competitive. Suddenly I'm not the know-it-all nerd. I'm not special. Everything I had going for me is gone. I feel I have no family, no school, no friends, no life.

Then I meet a person who gets me involved in the gang scene. There're always members willing to accept any lost kid. I don't join an African-American gang. I join a Chinese gang close to my new home.

A lot of Asian gangs are well hidden. The culture is closed and conservative. It's harder for the police to penetrate the community.

In Chinese gangs at that time, the girls do the less dangerous stuff, drive the getaway car, do the shoplifting, trash the places. The killings, the hideous crimes, are committed by the guys.

It's a patriarchal society. Girls are sex objects, valued for their looks. The guys steal for them, then wrap them around their finger. The girls are a prize.

Because of my tomboy upbringing, I'm more aligned with the guys. They call me a spitfire. Also back in my old 'hood, the girls are just as tough as the guys. If you say something a girl doesn't like, she'll smack you back. No reservation. That's the attitude I have and the way I behave.

Some of the guys are shocked. In the Asian culture, women tend to be more submissive. Of course, all people have limits, and when they pass a certain line, they'll blow up.

I start to lead a triple life. I play so many different roles I worry I might lose track. At home I am Mommy's good little girl. At school I'm the responsible student who always does her homework. In the gang I vent all my frustration and anger. I scream. I fight. I pick on people just because they look easy.

And I fall in love.

His name is Joe.

I am beginning to fool around with drugs. I experiment with marijuana. Joe sees me and throws me against the wall. He looks me straight in the eye and says, "My mother died of a drug overdose. I don't spend time with girls who do drugs. If I ever catch you using that stuff again, I'll personally kill you."

The way Joe says it, the way he looks at me, I believe him. And coming from a dysfunctional family, a dysfunctional environment, I know that violence and threats are the way people show that they care.

He cares about me! That's what he's telling me.

the difference

Although I hung around those gang members, a few things made me realize I was different. During that time, all the girls sprayed their hair, like, two feet high. I was allergic to hair spray. If I tried to use it, I'd sneeze and get terrible rashes.

All the girls in the gang used tons of makeup. My mom wouldn't allow me to use it ever. It was hard to sneak it, so usually I didn't bother.

I dressed differently, too. They dressed in all black. Even though I wore a lot of black, I liked variety. Often I had on some color. Also I didn't cut school that much. In fact, I liked school.

I didn't realize what being different would mean until one time we were finishing ruining someone's yard. Somebody yelled "Cops."

We all started running down the street. The police kept getting closer and closer. I didn't know what to do. Coming to a corner, I realized, "I don't look like the others."

Once we rounded the corner, I stopped cold, as the others kept running. I turned around and started to walk back toward the police and their cars. My heart was racing. But I walked slowly, very slowly, down the street. The police ran right by me. Some of the gang members got caught. I didn't.

And then Joe got killed.

To this day I don't know all the details. All I know is

he was shot in the back of the head. Okay. So he was running away. The police had no right to shoot him. I think he broke into a car or something like that and a police officer caught him.

The officer told him not to run, and he ran.

For a long time before that I thought, "I'm too smart and too slick for the cops to catch." I saw my friends get caught, but I was convinced it would never happen to me. I would never have a record. But when Joe died, he didn't have a police record either.

That was the first and the last time anybody ever caught him. "Wake up and smell the coffee," I told myself. "Get out before it's too late."

Of course, my mother knew nothing about this. I wasn't even supposed to be dating. How could I tell her I had a boyfriend, and now he was dead? I had to sneak to the funeral.

the break

I no longer knew which one was the true me: Mommy's girl, good student, or gang member. There was pressure to come back to the gang. There were also my memories of peer pressure to do the right thing. I missed my friends Derek and Amber and Joe.

"I need time," I told the gang members. "I have to get past the grief."

"Life goes on," they said. "We're here for you."

I knew I didn't want to be stuck at home, a failure,

> What would you do if the only people who understand you are the people you are running away from?

doing McDonald's labor. Instead I would hide myself under piles of work. I would focus on school.

I enter ninth grade at one of the best high schools in the city. Students at West High use SAT words. That's how they speak. That's what gets them the A's in class. I achieve academically. I read books. *Malcolm X, The Great Gatsby, One Hundred Years of Solitude.* Some of them are difficult, but I read them.

I begin to make friends. There's one girl in particular, a girl named Karen. Her family is well-off. Her parents care about her and her future. My father has disappeared. My mother is emotionally absent. I am the adult in the family. I try to open up to Karen, but then I realize I can't.

She has no idea what I'm talking about. She doesn't know what it is to be on the street.

At home at night, I argue with myself: "I have to go back to the gang. Everybody there will understand.

"But I don't want to go back. I want to cut myself away from that life."

There is no one I can ask, "What would you do if the only people who understand you are the people you are running away from?" For a whole year that battle rages inside me.

the extended family

I'm a junior in high school now. My grades are high. I will go to college.

I'm outgoing. I know a lot of people. I suppose I'm considered popular. Every day I have some different meeting, peer counselors, the Student Government Association, the city-sponsored Youth Advisory Council.

I don't discriminate. I have friends who support me in different ways. I can never tell the students at West about my past, but we relate in other important ways.

The Youth Advisory Council includes teenagers with troubled lives, ex-gang members to foster children. Sometimes we talk about our pasts. Listening to them is therapeutic for me.

I tell them, "No matter what my future brings, I know

this for a fact: You can take the girl out of the projects, but you can't take the projects out of the girl."

I can never change my past. My friends from those days will always be part of me. Some of them have dropped out of school. Some are in jail. Some are raising their own children. The last time I see Derek, he has his GED.

Then there's Amber, my religious neighbor who convinced us kids to let a bee live. One day I'm taking a shortcut to school. Amber's on the street corner. She's skinny. You can tell she's on drugs. It's obvious she's trying to sell her body.

She says, "Hey, Lola. Can you spare a couple bucks?"

I look at her and I think about luck. The gift of knowledge and education. I don't know the things that make her stand on the other side and me on this side. All I know is I got here and I'm thankful.

I give her my lunch money and go to school.

What do you think?

"You might think you're independent units running around. You can do what you want. But once you get into a gang, it's like a strong stream that carries you along. Even though you may feel you're swimming and making progress, much of the force is what your friends exert on you.

"Gangs mobilize around violence. It creates a sense of a tight organization against an outside threat. Because gang members have been ignored by most adults around them, they use this way to create a family of their own.

"Peers can shelter and support you through rough times. You need adults, though, to guide you. Look for somebody who's done well, who's been through what you've been through. Usually those people are approachable. Ask them for help."

—Tom Dishion, Ph.D., clinical psychologist,
Oregon Social Learning Center, Adolescent
Transitions Program, Eugene

with thanks

During the sixteen months I spent researching and writing this book, my family and friends offered continual support. Many thanks to my partner, Stan Mack, for his editing and design advice and counsel. Peter Mack helped as well with his QuarkXPress skills. Thanks, too, to Barbara Bode, Carolyn Bode, Lucy Cefalu, Jeanne Dougherty, Harriet Gottfried, Ted Gottfried, Ernie Lutze, Frieda Lutze, Carole Mayedo, Marvin Mazor, Rosemarie Mazor, Michael Sexton, and the Third Thursday Writers Group.

The following people provided me with valuable assistance:

Naomi Angier, young adult services coordinator, Multnomah County Library System, Portland, Oregon

Susan Dunn, young adult services coordinator, Salem Public Library, Salem, Oregon

Jean Dwyer, media specialist, Henninger High School, Syracuse, New York

Linda French, Rebecca Olmstead, media specialists, Springbrook High School, Silver Spring, Maryland

Susan Geiger, media specialist, Moreau Catholic High School, Hayward, California

Janet Gelfand, Sybil Oster, media specialists, Lawrence Middle School, Lawrence, New York

Pat Gordon, young adult services coordinator, Jackson County Library System, Medford, Oregon

Doris Griffin, media specialist, Smith School, Ramsey, New Jersey

Erin Hayden, media specialist, Laurel High School, Laurel, Maryland

Robin Hogans, special education teacher, Cardozo High School, Bayside, New York

Clara Johnson, media specialist, Terry Parker High School, Jacksonville, Florida

Jane Jury, media specialist, Elkton High School, Elkton, Maryland

Beverly Lee, young adult librarian, Douglas County Library System, Roseburg, Oregon

Tally Negroni, media specialist, Stamford High School, Stamford, Connecticut

Mike Printz, media specialist (retired), Topeka West High School, Topeka, Kansas

Charlie Reed, professor, chairperson, Education Department, University of North Carolina at Asheville, Asheville, North Carolina

Nadine Sarlin, media specialist, Locust Valley Junior-Senior High School, Locust Valley, New York

Bonnie Savitz, media specialist, Canarsie High School, Brooklyn, New York

Caryn Sipos, coordinator young adult services, Alameda County Library, Fremont, California

Raya Then, media specialist, Williamsville Public Library, Williamsville, New York

And, of course, a special thank you to my editor, Kathleen Squires, and to the individual teenagers who volunteered to share their stories. If those students hadn't been willing to open their lives, this book would not exist.

about the author

JANET BODE writes hard-hitting nonfiction books for and about teenagers, including the Delacorte Press titles *Death Is Hard to Live With* and *Heartbreak and Roses*. Through group discussions and one-on-one interviews, she uncovers the personal stories behind today's headlines and then reports them to her readers. Several of her books, including *The Voices of Rape: Healing the Hurt; New Kids on the Block: Oral Histories of Immigrant Teens*, and *Beating the Odds: Stories of Unexpected Achievers*, have been selected Best Books for Young Adults. Her book *Different Worlds: Interracial and Cross-Cultural Dating* was made into a CBS-TV *Schoolbreak Special*.